Hack Writer:

pOemS   stories   Plays

Dan Sklar

ISBN: 0-75961-193-9

This book is printed on acid free paper.

1stBooks – rev. 4/10/01

For Stanley and Elaine

Contents

Poems

Going To The Opera.. 1

14 May 2000 3

The Importance Of Sweat.. 5

Themes.. 7

Beautiful Mystery 9

Doing Nothing 11

Silence 13

Whisper... 14

Wanting 15

Galatea 16

Numbers And Love... 17

Writer's Block 18

A Poem 19

Little Poem 20

Robert Frost's Bones 21

Kjihp... 22

The Importance Of Sweat.. 23

Gray 24

Two Dreams 25

Sam Listens... 27

Teacher, My Son Is Not A Robot 28

October 30

There Are Some Things You Have To Do 31

Canoes 32

One Great Poem.. 33

The Truth About The Beats 35

It Is Something To Be A Hack 36
April 15, 1998 38
March 23, 1998 41
To Live And Mean It 43
November 28, 1997 46
Canoe On An Old River 49
Clio 50
Sammy's Sleeping Arrangements 51
January 9, 2000 52
An Afternoon In The Life Of A 9 Year Old 53
Unitarian Girls 54
Longing For You 56
Rugged 57
Forty-Five 59
The Circus 60
Academic Excellence 61
Angels 63
A Winter Night 65
Lucky Strikes 67
John Steinbeck On The Corner 68
Feet Feet 70
What Is It About Moby Dick? 71
Nature Is Its Own Poem 73
Poetry Rewards And Honors And Literary Prizes 74
Fish 75
Laughing Buddha, Vincent Ferrini 76
One Day 78
March 30, 2000 80
Jazz On Saturday, March 4, 2000 81
Fifty-One Haiku 83

The Essential Tool Box 90

This Settles The Abraham & Isaac & God Thing 91

The Kid 92

How To Be Forty-Six 93

Godzilla An Epic Poem 97

Old Men 98

(Three Found Poems From *Public Speaking* Principles And
    Practice) 99

Why? 101

Buster Keaton Running 102

Buster Keaton 103

A Paranoid Middle-Aged Professor 104

Sonnet To Duse 107

Zen 108

No Time Even To Write This Crummy Poem 110

Anger 112

Night Rain Fire Pond Beat 113

Paddle Slowly 115

Paper 116

March Winds 118

My Poetry 120

Rain 121

Baseball Is 122

Red Sox June 12, 1998 123

My Sports 124

Stories

The Paperboy 125

Scotch And Love And Adultery 132

Plays

Siberian Women And The Red Moon 141

The Day Frank Sinatra Died 253

Going To The Opera

I am going to the opera.
I'm off to the opera.
She went to the opera.
He went to the opera.
The opera always seems
like a good place to be
going to and to have been
and to be there away
from someplace else.
It is good when someone
says of you that you are
at the opera or that you
have been to the opera.
Your kids can say dad
and mom went to the opera.
I mean, what is it about
the opera that it is a good
place to be going or to be
there or to have been?
For one thing, you must
take a shower before going
and put on clean clothes
and dress up very neatly.
It is good to be clean
with other clean people.
Some women wear perfume.
It smells good and reminds you
of your second grade teacher.
The men usually shave and slap
on after-shave lotion and their
face tingles to them.
I like to wear argyle socks
and a white shirt and striped

Dan Sklar

tie and blue suit like in prep
school and I am still in the
habit. Another good thing
about the opera is you go to
dinner somewhere and
the silverware sparkles and
the thick cotton napkin is heavy
on your whole lap. You go to
the opera with someone you love.
She wears a black dress and you
look at her beautiful shoulders.

14 May 2000

Max asked me
if I ever teased
a kid or stood up
for a kid.
We were driving
to my office
to print something.
I told him
a never teased
anyone and it
was the truth.
Then I said
I stood up
for a black
kid once.
I was eating a
chocolate cupcake
and a French kid
with black hair
and a high-pitched
laugh said
the cake was made
out of the black
kid's skin.
I punched the French
kid right in the face
and got in
trouble for it.
The black kid
was sad and
we never talked
about it.
Max said I did

the right thing,
but nowadays
people don't
punch kids-
they tell the teacher.

Themes

These are images
that keep cropping
up in my poetry:
Tree roots that bust
up sidewalk pavement,
a plain sandwich,
a woman's shoulders,
the music of Ray
Anthony especially
"Harlem Nocturne"
and "At Last." (Only
because that is what
I am listening to as I
write this. But really
any jazz if you look.)
Max on the saxophone,
Sammy dancing on the
table and making a
museum. Denise
with long legs and
sharp chin, all grace.
Bicycles and canoes
and drums and canoes
and bicycles and drums,
losing, sweating,
being mediocre, third-rate,
getting rejected, getting
taken advantage of and
knowing it and letting
it happen and liking it,
rusted Radio Flyer,
things left outside all
year, old-fashioned

romance, September
nights and stars.

Beautiful Mystery

I want my kids
to know the beauty
of the world.
The fact that
at nine years old
my son plays
Mamillius in
The Winter's Tale
means nothing
to educational
research and
analysis and testing
which do not
answer the
questions because
they are the wrong
ones and do not
have anything to
do with
the beautiful mystery
of spirit and mind.
You can organize
and categorize and
test and never see
the beautiful mystery
that cannot be
tested or organized or
categorized or researched
or analyzed or statisticized.
What is important is
what is beautiful is my
kid in a Shakespeare play
and my other kid loving

Dan Sklar

and not getting enough
of the Greek Myths and
the fact that they both
love Louis Armstrong.

Doing Nothing

It is good to go to your own office and do nothing.

Sit in your chair and look around at the things.

Maybe pull out a book called *Von Stroheim*

and look at the pictures of ZaSu Pitts as Trina,

and put your feet up on the desk and maybe look

at old poems you wrote and think hey they're not

bad. Oh, well, it does no good really to admire

your own work. Out the window in the hall

there's a great boulder across the street

with a "One Way" sign in front of it.

There's Emily Dickinson and Hemingway and

Stanislavsky and *Public Speaking Principles*

and Practice with photo of Wendell Willkie

and Carl Sandburg and John L. Lewis and

labor leaders a subject which has been on

your mind lately. You think you should have

been a Union organizer or a Frank Norris

11

Dan Sklar

scholar and you want to get in a fight with the

bosses because you don't like the way they

treat people and you just want to get in a fight

because and because is a good enough reason

when your heart is pumping and you are hungry.

Silence

I have failed in my own silence,

in the silence of snowshoes,

in north silence, in canoe silence

and nights stars winters silence.

I have failed in the silence

of water and sky and voices.

Dan Sklar

Whisper

I want

to whisper

something

to her.

Something

about her

face says

whisper

to me.

Wanting

I always wanted to be

great at something—

a great actor,

a great novelist,

a great lawyer,

a great something,

a great teacher,

a great poet,

a great artist,

a great scholar,

a great father,

a great husband,

a great lover,

a great playwright,

a great jazz drummer.

Galatea

I have been thinking about Cleopatra
and Kim Novak and Galatea and how
Jimmy Stewart waited and thought
about Kim Novak in *Vertigo* I don't
believe any of it except his obsession
and how he is desperate and how his
vertigo made him free. That world of
San Francisco in the fifties movie color
and the redwood trees and the bridge
and the Mission with the fake horse.
I mean I feel I can sink into that kind
of deep sadness without the guilt and
it is how Jimmy Stewart as Johnny is
leaving places and going to places and
thinking and there is a student in my
class who looks like how I picture
Cleopatra with big eyes and sharp
features and bright mystery in her
And it is the story of Galatea I think
of and how Pygmalion carved her
and some stories say it was his prayers
to Venus that did it and others say it
was how the statue reminded Venus
of herself and all the stories have him
bringing little flowers and dressing
the statue I mean he prayed for a
maiden like her you know and Venus
gave him her alive and named her
Galatea which means sleeping love.

Numbers and Love

I do not understand numbers.

I think that numbers come

between us because love has

nothing to do with numbers

except for how long we have

loved each other.

If we didn't know the numbers

would we love each other any less?

If we did not know what

we earned would we love

each other any less?

If we forgot all the numbers

we know and ever knew

the answer would be the same.

Dan Sklar

Writer's Block

Either I have writer's

block or no time to write

I'm not sure which.

And I cannot figure

out if I have any ideas

or not, but I think I do.

It occurs to me that

I want to be walking

alone in a blizzard, thinking

about being in a tea room

alone with you. I don't mean

I want to do this, but I want

to want to do this while

walking in a snow storm.

A Poem

I do not want anybody

to know my name.

I want to be an actor

in a movie drunk at a bar

because the woman I love

doesn't love me—

remember it is a movie

and I am an actor

and nobody knows

my name.

I meet a sweaty

and dirty woman.

Dan Sklar

Little Poem

I do not want

a name anymore.

I want to hear

sleeping

and rain

and spring wind

and sudden

spring rain

so cool

my name will

never matter.

Robert Frost's Bones

I am more interested in
Robert Frost's bones
than in his poems.
Here's how it is—Saturday
there was going to be this
Robert Frost conference
in Lawrence so I asked
some of my students
to go and report back
to the class and to swipe
one of Robert Frost's bones
that'd be on display there
so I could pull it out when
we read Frost's poems.
It was a big joke but I was
serious that's why it was
funny but they believed it
at first because I am more
interested in his bones
than I am in his poems.
The way I see it, that fella
stopped by the woods to eat
a bologna sandwich and
smoke an Old Gold cigarette
which tastes pretty good
when it's snowing
in the woods.

Dan Sklar

kjihp
Sammy Sklar 4

Sammy is not interested

in Barbie he likes super

heroes power toys he

plays with them and then

he walks on the sidewalk

and eats a tuna sandwich

which tastes better in the fall

with wind and leaves flying

off of the trees and they're

really crunchy and then

he walks on the sidewalk

again to get some Juicy Fruit.

the end

The Importance of Sweat
Maxfield Sklar 9

Spit on it. It's too

neat. It's nice cool and very

clean. Spit on it now.

Dan Sklar

Gray
Maxfield Sklar 6

Gray, gray the color of a confederate soldier

Gray, gray the color of a rock.

Gray, gray the color of a cobblestone.

And also the color of a shirt,

A hat and an elephant.

Gray, the feeling of a whoosh of air,

the feeling of a man.

Two Dreams

Sammy fills my hat with pebbles
I sweep the brick patio we play
in the hammock and he makes me
laugh with his crazy dances and jokes
and I make him laugh like I make
Maxfield laugh with our vaudeville
routines like Fred Allen and Steve Allen
and we listen to Count Basie and Nat
Simpkins I dream of playing drums
with Max on the saxophone and Sam
maybe on the trombone and I think
about the faces where I work and am
suddenly interested in faces not really
suddenly but some of the faces I cannot
get out of my head even when I am with
them and I want sometimes to write deep
and profound and philosophical poems
with metaphors and images and the works
and I get hypnotized by faces and eyes
because I look at them I mean I forget
myself and look at them and forget to
forget what I forget two dreams last night
you were in one but you were my cousin
too because you have the same face
but your face has haunted me for two years
Sure this ain't no E. Dickinson or R. Frost
or T.S. Eliot or W.C.W poem I wonder if
W.C Fields ever read W.C Williams poems?
and my wife gave me cross-country skis
for my fortieth birthday that was six years
ago and I have used them twice but I
dreamed I was in Manhattan in a cross-
country ski shop and the city was empty

and it was us and one other customer
and you were the saleswoman and in
the city I wanted to go to a cross-country
ski lodge with you in the dream and now
in the other dream I was in a store where
no one spoke English and I was trying to
call you but no one understood me and it
was night and old and people sat at tables
in dark clothes and wore hats and I had
to call you because your face and eyes
are like some great white jungle cat.

Sam Listens

I want to write about Samuel
and the time he stood
on the front lawn
on a warm April day
and it was six p.m.
and there were birds
and bells and a train
whistle and bees
and a dog and an airplane
and a car and kids playing
and ball bouncing
and wind chimes
and lawn mower and distant
piano and a mother calling
"Ronny!"
A hammering somewhere.
I want to write this poem
to remember the time when
Sam was one year
and three months listening
to these things that
came all at once.
To see Sam in a
white tee-shirt,
white diaper, bare feet,
Finger pointing to the air,
Mouth saying something.

Dan Sklar

Teacher, My Son is Not a Robot

At the parent teachers meeting

I did not speak.

My son's teachers were not talking

about the boy I know.

They were talking about a boy

they want to be like the rest.

They talked about a boy

who is not a robot, and that

is what they want, robots.

They did not talk about the boy

who acts out the stories we read.

The red ants crawl all over him

and he is sinking in quicksand

and he is Queequeg with a shrunken

head and Pip at Magwich's death

bed and George telling Lenny about

the rabbits. So his math is not perfect

and he writes some letters backwards,

but *man* can he read and his poems

are poetry and they made the teachers

cry (one of them anyway).

That was all I needed to hear.

Dan Sklar

OCTOBER

October calls to my blood
To go with an actors troupe
in wagons and horses
To towns in New England
valleys that are the taste
of apples which touch
the top of wagons and we
pick as we pass and bite into.
We set up the stage in the wind,
leaves fly around our horses.
We put on costumes—
great gypsy costumes and rags
and princes and kings and
princesses and queens and we
become them with grand
and simple lines and press
our faces together and breathe
in each others breaths and
October air and fight and run
into great embraces and there
are flashes of violence with
October afternoon sun across
trees and faces and swords
and faces of the people who
are with us in their imaginations
in our play, our play…
Oh, it is good to long for a girl
I can never have
To see her face,
in the audience,
loving me.

There are Some Things You Have to Do

This is the way it is when a guy says "Wanna step outside?"
You have no choice. You have to go outside and you
have to say, "All right, let's go right now." And in your
mind you are willing and ready to accept the fact that
your teeth might get knocked out and your nose busted,
or maybe since he is always a giant, he'll be slow
and lumbering and you can dive, fists flying at his face
and all the time your wife is saying, "Let's just leave."
But you cannot, it is impossible, something in your
bones and blood and brain tells you in no uncertain
terms that you have to do this thing. Your eyes tighten,
your fists become rocks, your skin and muscles harden
in a flash and the truth is you have it in you to kill
a man because you are designed that way. Your
wife hates it and loves it and hates it and loves it
and hates it and loves it and hates it and loves it.
Nine times out of ten he will back down
because he senses and sees and knows you
have snapped and someday, someday, someday,
your son will walk around your backyard
in the rain shivering and talking and grabbing
toys to mess with and will not come into the house
and he will like being wet and cold getting on his
tricycle and playing with an old fishing rod.
And someday you will be canoeing with your
boy on a river and he will not want to stop and
you two will shout at the river and trees and rocks
and sky and silence with big mouths and hats
pulled way down over your eyes and he will turn
to you and say, "This is nice, Dad, really nice."

31

Dan Sklar

CANOES

The Iroquois traveled in canoes
Paddles dipped into green water
Birch-bark reflected white and black.
I have been thinking about canoes
Since I drifted alone on Emerald Pond
Since I glided along the shore of Long Pond
White dots glittered across to still rocks,
To the line of deep green, thick on the edge
Where tree meets tree until death.
What is it about canoes that draw me?
As a kid I canoed down the Delaware River
We tipped it over on purpose on the rapids
We camped on the riverbank under stars
I forget the longing in the sleeping bag.
Why are canoes on my mind?
Why do I think about canoes
When I am late for a train to Boston
When a bill is past due
When the baby doesn't sleep nights
When I have a hundred compositions to mark?

ONE GREAT POEM

I want to write one great poem
that will win one of the contests
in *Poets & Writers Magazine.*
They will put in a little photograph
of me, half smiling or not smiling.
(A photographer once told me that I
looked better when I did not smile.)
The magazine will write little things
about me being a promising writer
even though I am forty-five
and the promises
have already been kept.
I want to write just one great poem
that college students will either get
or not get or hate or puzzle over
and write papers about with thesis
sentences and all that and misread
and read right to help them be wise.
I want high school valedictorians
to recite it at commencements.
Everyone will nod and say,
"Yes, yes, it is so true, so true."
But they will not really be sure
they know exactly
what is true about it.
But it will sound true and they
will sense that it is true and wise.
That will be enough.
I will be asked to speak at small
colleges in Indiana
and upstate New York.
I will look for profound
things to say and read my

33

one great poem
and it will be enough.

The Truth About the Beats

Did you ever think that maybe the Beat poets were not so great
and that it was all just a stream of consciousness trick that
sounds good because the lonely images strike us and the
thoughts of one human being jammed on pages with words I
suppose is poetry enough to readers and listeners half reading
and half listening because who listens to poetry wholly really
come on let's face it poetry is small potatoes, peanuts, it's the
cheap side show, the menagerie they banned but anyone who
saw one will not forget the giant sitting there looking slow and
fleshy and sad on his big chair as people streamed by staring
streaming like the stream of images and thoughts and what was
the giant thinking in his giant brain with his big heavy lips as
thick as swollen giant lips.

But oh the stream of consciousness poets love to light cigarettes
in the dark and howl at the moon and climb trees to the stars
and stand in shadows in trench coats in the night alone in
doorways of cheap Chinese Restaurants like good bad detective
novels on the trail of something always yourself and the girl like
Veronica Lake with saxophone music always John Coltrane or
Charlie Parker maybe Miles Davis or Dizzy Gillespie never
Louis Armstrong or Count Basie and it is never middle-aged
with kids for some odd reason somehow the amazing miracle of
kids never quite got to the Beats except for maybe Gary Snyder
but he doesn't count as a Beat because, well, just because, and
the small compact beautiful miracle missed them.

Oh, sure it is swell to be in a smoky café reading and smoking
and writing in a million journal books and driving on America
and all that, but nothing beats, I mean nothing beats it when your
kid keeps a journal and you read it and it says, "I am happy."

It is Something to be a Hack

What do you do if you write plays
and you go to a reading of one
and you realize you will never be great?
You want to be great but you haven't
the talent so you have to live
as a third-rate playwright. I mean
the people laugh but what does it mean?
People laughing after a while means
very little because all they remember
is that they laughed and the play
was funny but it was missing something.
I mean they may even chuckle at some
lines now and then, but they do that
from TV shows and maybe you wanted
more than that, though even being a
hack writer is something to get to and I
have arrived with my eleven manuscripts,
eleven scripts bound neatly with good titles.
My wife says I write good titles:
Human Nature,
Demolition and Construction,
Teachers who Smoke Cigarettes,
Everybody Wants to be Pocahontas,
The At Last Hotel,
The Day Frank Sinatra Died,
Modern Drama,
The Revolution of the Muses,
Siberian Women and the Red Moon,
Scotch and Love and Adultery,
Unitarian Girls.
Where does it end?
What does it mean to be third-rate
and know it in your bones and

sometimes tortured by it?
To know the limit of your talent
and to know that if it mattered
it may not help because at forty-five
in 1999 I can say I am a hack writer;
and the eleven scripts are placed in an even
pile on the floor by my nine year old son
who reads pieces of them, stacks them,
looks through them and says, "Dad,
I am going to put these on the bookshelf."

Dan Sklar

April 15, 1998

What is this feeling when I get a call
from my old headmaster I haven't seen
in thirty years and he leaves a message
on the machine, his voice, the same
saying he and his wife will be
at the Tremont House Hotel in Boston and
would I meet them for a drink there
at five o'clock? I leave a message
to confirm that I will be there Wednesday
so I arrange to have my mother-in-law
watch the boys because Denise is teaching
and I shine my shoes waiting for the train
because my old headmaster was a Marine,
Special Services, and he was a disciplinarian
authoritarian type but a good one that we
respected because deep inside we knew
he was like that for our own good and this
night thirty years later I discover we were
right and it was true he was looking out
for our own good because in this world
someone has to. The last time I saw him
was the time when I was hauled into his
office for punching my roommate
in the eye. My headmaster, I could tell,
pretended to be angry when he asked me
why I did it and I lied and he didn't believe
me but he didn't say so, so we let it
go at that. All the boys loved his wife
because she seemed to be real and motherly,
but not too much.
I told them how I remembered everything,
I mean everything about my old prep
school days. I would always be fourteen

to them until this night when now I am
a middle-aged, balding man, slightly
beefy, cheerful, somewhat successful
as an associate professor and poet, playwright,
husband and father, but still that quiet
friendly boy who sometimes got in trouble
in a good way and didn't smoke and
played baseball and always shot doubles
into center field even though he used to
say he couldn't figure out how I got hits
standing the way I did and how could
I catch balls when I always stepped in,
not back, and the balls flew over my head
and it was a miracle when I did actually
catch one and it was always a miracle to
me too. I ran down what I knew happened
to my old prep school pals who were still my pals
and about their successes, their wives and work and
divorces and remarriages and parents.
They told me how our teachers then were
teachers to get out of the draft to keep from
getting blown apart in Vietnam.
(In college, a few years later, my draft lottery
number was 284. I don't know what I would
have done if I was drafted.
I know I didn't want to have my legs
blown off or be a hero and there was no
Hitler to fight. In fact, Ho Chi Min was a
Jeffersonian Republican so there was
something fishy about dying for it all.)
But here I was, now, in the bar of the Tremont
House Hotel, and I'm feeling that
as he is about to retire in June and I am
in the middle of it all, that there is
something right and good and decent
about the way we conducted ourselves

and here we are having scotch on the rocks together,
(She had a glass of wine). I told them some
of my inner thoughts and they told me
some of theirs and since then I do not dream
about those prep school years anymore.

March 23, 1998

The floors are wearing out in my house.
The books and scrap papers pile up.
Sam brings me *Good Hunting, Blue Sky*
to read to him. He likes the forest.
I don't know how the characters
will end my play, *The Day Sinatra Died.*
I like that title.
Max keeps a record of the times
Denise and I argue—seventeen since
he started. He and his friends tear through
the house slamming into each other
tugging each other, throwing each other
around. I am saving up for that
transistor short wave radio from the
catalogue. I do a poetry radio program
Saturday mornings. I don't know
what it is about radio…. I like the
rejection slips the magazines send when
they send back my poems. I like how my
play *The At Last Hotel* loses play contests.
I like how Sam pulls out board games
and throws the pieces around the room—
Monopoly tokens, the ship, the shoe,
the racing car, the thimble, dice, deeds,
the paper money, white and blue and pink.
I like how he climbs on the table
and throws the napkins on the floor.
I like how the car needed an alternator
and it wrecked our budget.
(I can't remember when our budget
wasn't wrecked.) I like how it snows
the second day of spring. I like
how Sam builds towers with blocks,

Dan Sklar

knocks them down then builds them
again and knocks them down and
builds them again.

To Live and Mean It

It is strange to be in the house
Sam asleep upstairs, Max and Denise
at rehearsal. Friday night.
I don't know what to do first.
I walk through the house—thinking.
Plan classes? Read something?
Write something? Finish watching
the 1948 Jimmy Cagney movie
with William Bendix, Saroyan's
The Time of Your Life I started
in April 1997?
It is now January 1998.
I look at the years poets were born.
Odd to see the ones born the same
year as me, 1953, and the blank place
for the year of death.
I want to write something with a part one
and part II, but each can stand alone.
I'll record part II; people will listen.
It is quiet strange here, no one around,
Sam could be up at any second.
I put on a tape of poetry and think
that when the poets read their own work
what once seemed profound in the poems
is contrived and does not seem important.
Maybe I hate poetry—some of it, but then
Theodore Roethke reads—
and hell it is great.
Boy, could he read and mean it
and write and mean it
and live and mean it.
I need to be alone first to live
and mean anything and be any good.

Say, you know, I sent a proposal
to deliver a paper at a big deal,
very important type conference
(on reflection, for crying out loud)
of the National Council of Teachers of English
(I used to get their unreadable magazine).
In the proposal I proposed to talk about
the idea and concept and thing about
reading and thinking in solitude.
Man, did they hate it. The thing about
being alone was not in their lexicon, I guess.
They couldn't stand the fact that before you
can get into a group and talk about anything
you might need to come to grips with being alone
to do nothing or something and think seriously
or silly about anything alone in the real human
solitude you need to come up with anything independently.
You can't teach independent thinking
without teaching independent thinking;
and you probably can't teach it anyway.
The more scholars use sources and quotes
and statistics and citations and references
and case studies, the more I don't agree
with them even if I happen to agree with them;
and the more I believe in dreams.
The slicker their schedules and Doubletree
Hotels in Seattle and photographs of scholars
smiling and looking quite pleased with themselves
the quicker I canceled my membership.
That showed them!
I tell you their literature is making the trees nervous.
It dawned on me that I am not a scholar anyway.
I mean, if I was born in Lithuania
I would still be a house painter, but
this is America, so I am a college professor.
My kids don't care if I am not a scholar;

my wife doesn't care; and my boss sort of
doesn't care. It doesn't matter to the milkshakes
I make for Max and Sam. It doesn't matter to me
when I see the poetry in Sam, two years old,
playing with two pieces of white paper
on a chair in the living room.

Dan Sklar

November 28, 1997

It is 6:30 A.M. and I have a half hour before
Maxfield and Samuel and Denise wake up.
I have to make Max's lunch, tuna fish,
play with Sam and talk to Denise.
I have to drive Max to school and then
go to work. Read student poems, write
final exams, mark compositions, plan classes,
read stories and poems and *Romeo and Juliet.*
I have been writing in several different
notebooks. I write in the first few pages,
the rest stay blank. I have ideas for plays
and poems and stories, but my kids
come first and when they come first
I give them all of my attention energy.
There is nothing left for writing work.
The rest goes to teaching work
because teaching work
is paying work—the work
I chose and wanted.
It is the work that came from the voice
I heard since I can remember.
Be a teacher.
Now I feel delight in every teacherly task—
even the painful ones.
The refrigerator hums,
the kettle on the stove shines,
the news is on the radio. I have twenty minutes left.
There are apples and pears and bananas
and a cup of black coffee on the counter.
I think about cross country skiing,
oil heat, house shingles, and how Samuel
likes lollipops and Maxfield likes the Civil War;
Denise and kisses and no kisses.

Sammy is two. He draws circles and dots
and lines and listens to Johnny Mercer
and plays with matchbox cars, puzzles, and water.
Max is seven. He sounds out words
and is beginning to get math.
My book, *Straightforward*, with the cover
photograph of my grandfather, Max,
the best part of the book with old
stories and stories I left out and lines
I cut and plays with vaudeville jokes
nobody knows anymore anyway.
I think about my dear Uncle Stanley.
One or two obsessions each semester-
someone I can't quit thinking about
who becomes a character in a play
and has bedroom eyes.
The Paul Revere pots and pans
hang on the wall over the stove.
They were a wedding present seventeen
years ago. The November 1997 calendar
is on the wall. I can see "The Torn Hat"
painting my mother painted.
"The best part of Legos,"
says Max, "is putting them together."
The best part of life is putting it together.
"Do you have to get married," he hollered
in the middle of running across the field
in a soccer game. "I want to live in this house
when I grow up." At 44, I realize why
my friend's father was taciturn.
Ten minutes to go.
My desk will be a changing table
for another year.
I like to write lists of things to do
and cross them out when they are done.
I write ideas for characters and poems

but the ones in my head are the only
ones that get anywhere.
Some of the top stories in the news comes on.
I like that phrase, the top stories.
What are the top stories in this house?
My sons, Max and Sam, are the top stories.
Five minutes, no four and a half until
I smell the sleep of my boys.
When I sit down to read, Sam says,
"Daddy, you read a book," and he pulls
Go, Dog. Go! from the shelf and looks
for the "Do you like my hat" pages.
He plows through a dozen books,
stands up and takes my hand to pull
me to the next thing-the next task-
the next thing on the list. He is Mr. Smily—
Mr. Twink guy- Sammy Guy.
I think of Max and some of his coloring books:
Heroines of the Civil War, Ancient Greeks,
Heroines of The American Revolution,
Ancient India, New England Authors,
Macbeth, Ships, Ancient China, Black Authors,
Billy Yank, Johnny Reb, Ancient Japan,
Native American Designs.
It's seven o'clock. This life. This day.
Reveille then revelry.

Canoe on an Old River

There are no more places to send the things I write

I have reached my peak and the rest is listening to

jazz and playing drums and watching my kids grow

and getting a canoe to drift down some old river

and riding my bicycle to the library and store

making love with my wife when the kids are asleep

teaching my classes and getting the students to be

who they are and what's left for me to do is get

into this union thing and stand up for the weak

against the strong I love that quote about human

feelings in conflict with institutional things

because institutions save you and then destroy

you because there is no place for the individual

reading alone or drifting in a canoe on an old river.

Dan Sklar

CLIO

I figured out that you
are my muse and
I need a muse and
you look like Clio
the muse of history,
writing in your book
with your vivid eyes
and lines and arms.
I need a muse who
lives in my mind
in a beam of sun light
and that is how I see you,
will not get close to you
or think about you
any way but as a muse.
You walk down the hall
like a goddess in my mind
and every image I have
of you in your blonde
red longness and the scent
of you and the laugh of you
is for this poem.
There is something
wrapped tight about you
I would like to unwrap
slowly.
There is something
perfect in this
imagined innocence.

Sammy's sleeping arrangements
as of Jan. 11, 2000, his fourth birthday

These are all of the places
Sammy has slept.
Brothers Restaurant sitting
in my lap, head on the table,
the kitchen floor (with me),
the living room floor,
a booth at McDonald's,
the car, the café at the Aquarium
(I watched it snow on the green water),
the couch, on me, on the train,
the kitchen counter, and on Denise.
One year I slept on the floor,
every night, my feet up on the bed.
Now sometimes I sleep
with Sam or alone or with
Max in Max's bed or with Sam
in Sam's bed or alone or with
Max in Sam's bed and Denise
sleeps with Sam or Max or
Sam and Max or alone.
Sometimes I sleep with Denise.

January 9, 2000

Sammy rode with me on the tandem bicycle today.
He loved it and he will be four on Tuesday.
He did not want to go home. He loves staying
out nights and going places. We went to a
playground and he didn't want to leave.
It was good to be out in the cool air in January,
no snow on the ground, lights on in all of the
houses. I feel that the world is open now that
I can ride with Sammy on the tandem! Now
we can fly all over town and to the beach at
Winter Island. And when we come home Max
is practicing the saxophone and I watch him
from outside and he reads the music and my
heart soars. Sammy and I look at the crescent
moon through the trees above the rooftops and
Denise is cooking and talking to her sister Joan.

An Afternoon in the Life of a 9 Year Old
December 6, 1999

After school Maxfield
had a saxophone lesson.
At home, he practiced
saxophone, and I played
congas to keep time.
He practiced karate forms
and then did math and
spelling homework.
He wrestled with Sammy.
He practiced the recorder
in bed and said
he wanted to play a solo
of "Westminster Chimes."
He read a Hardy Boys Series
Crusade of the Flaming Sword
and went to sleep.

Unitarian Girls

What was the last thing he wrote

and where was it published?

This guy is dangerous.

Too big for his britches.

They listen to him.

He reads the contract.

What have we got on him?

Plenty.

What does he say?

"Have to side with the weak

against the strong."

What else does he say?

The people come around

and see he is right.

"Have to fight

to keep liberty.

To fight and never stop."

They want to make him

president of their association.

It's a union, he likes

to call it what it is.

Longing For You

I do not like poetry &
cannot stop writing it &
reading it & thinking about
it & I do not like the fact
that I want my poems in
Poetry & *APR.* This is
what I have to do today:
1. Long for you.
B. Long for you.
c. Long for you
IV. Long for you.

Rugged

The poems in *Poetry Magazine*
are dainty, that's the word—dainty
Even the poem with a man
looking at a woman's legs.
Too many flowers and regrets
and gardens and little churches
and music lessons and not
enough Malcolm X.
There aren't enough poems
that clobber you.
I been trying to tell you
If I told you once, I told
you a thousand times
my poetry is rugged.
I tell you it's rugged.
I walk around my house
declaring it is rugged.
I reckon my poetry
is rugged. It ain't dainty.
It's tough and rugged.
My wife says it's not
rugged. I say it is dog-eared,
worn-out, beat-up, dog-legged,
left in the rain, and rusting
in the backyard all winter.
It's a busted stone wall,
a falling down fence.
There is nothing academic
about it I hope.
I say my poetry is rugged
My kids say it's rugged too
because I tell them it is and
we all march through our house

saying it's rugged I tell you!
My wife says it's not.
I say it's a radio playing
in another room.
A car engine running
A cold February night
with Jupiter and Venus
and Mercury visible
from home.
It's me thinking about
the FBI file on Malcolm X
and eating Shabazz Bean Pie
in Harlem on the street
with a Kool Cigarette
in the cold city air
thinking about Thelonious Monk.
It is Malcolm X wounded
then dead.
The only way to be yourself
is to be yourself.
I lose and it is good.

FORTY-FIVE

What is it about
being in my forties?
If forties was a color
it would be brown.
Forty-five is like new
driftwood.
It is a red tree.
It is a shovel jammed
into a pile of earth.
It is dirt.
It is the ground.
It is walking with
my hands deep
in my pockets.
Forty-five is a sliver
of forest behind
old houses.
Forty-five is a cloudy
day when the
sun comes
out sometimes.
It is the shadow
of a red car.
It is a last romance
in my mind.
It is wanting to walk
to a train station
alone and to kiss
the shoulders of
a tall woman.

Dan Sklar

THE CIRCUS

Circuses are depressing.
The clowns rarely
make me laugh.
They are sad mostly
and get me thinking
about my life.
The acrobats seem
empty.
I do not believe
the sincerity
of the ringmaster.
The elephants
and sleek horses
and dogs
and tigers
are distracted,
mechanical—
something's wrong.
The tightrope artists
and trapeze artists
have perfected
their mistakes.
The beautiful girl
on the elephant
seems sad.
I would rather
watch a girl
alone writing
in her journal
under a tree.

Academic Excellence

Academic excellence is loving your bones
and the bones of your mother.
It is the moon and moss.
Academic excellence is moss
and bones and moon and
brain that knows what it knows
and does and thinks what it wants
and what it doesn't want.
What did academic excellence mean
to your feet and bones in your feet
when you were 3 and when you
were 23 and when you were 43?
It is moss and moon and night
and knowing the difference between
machines and love and moss
and moon and bones
and Mona Lisa and Louis Armstrong
and poetry and machines and Charlie Parker
and bones and love
and stars and night
and stars and stars
and conga drums
It is nothing good is ever over.
It is messing
with your 3 year old's bare feet
as you say bears, elephants,
crocodiles, giraffes, wolves,
coyotes, elephants, and tigers
and tigers because academic
excellence is tigers and tigers
and Louis Armstrong
and John Coltrane
and Vincent van Gogh

and Clio and Thalia and Duse
and moss and bones
and bones and moss.
and stars and love
and cigars and drums
and nights and nights
and rain and rain
and moss and bones.

ANGELS

This talk about angels it occurred to me
if I had one he would be an old Black man
like Louis Armstrong. A jazz musician
I bet. Count Basie maybe. Basie knew
when to blast the horns then touch one
piano key and it was art because you
never knew when it was coming and it
always came at the right moment.
I saw Basie's Big Band once--the one
white guy was the drummer--blonde hair,
white, white skin. Man did he swing.
I always watched the drummer at shows
for some reason. The snare drum, cymbals,
tom toms, and percussion things.
I practiced paradiddles on a red rubber pad
on a piece of wood and said these names:
Nat King Cole, Lester Young, Billie Holiday,
Thelonius Monk, Dinah Washington, Viola
Williams. The sound of these names! Viola
Williams was the cook at my prep school.
Always in a bad mood, let us raid the bread
at midnight, we liked the stale triangles of white
bread. She had dark chocolate skin, thick lips,
a real hourglass shape. It was 1968.
I think about her. She lived in an apartment
behind the kitchen in the old Merrill Estate
(that's the stock broker company Merrill
the house the poet James Merrill lived in
for a time as a kid). Funny how I lived
there too when I was in eighth grade. I
took a bath in the same bath as Merrill
and saw the same night and moon over
the potato fields behind the hedges. I

walked the same brick paths in the formal
gardens and breathed the same November
ocean. On winter Saturday nights Viola's
boyfriend would stay with her.
He wore a dark suit and hat.
He was short and sturdy and black
with a white Lucky Strike in his mouth.
His hands were dense and brown like
the ground. He came quietly and left
quietly and Viola was happy on Sundays.
I wonder if she still sees the man.
I wonder of they ever married.
Somehow I knew he took the train
from Brooklyn. I saw him once
walking from the station to the school,
hat pulled down. Cigarette.
What did he do sitting alone on the train?
What did he think about walking from
the station to the mansion where Viola
lived behind the kitchen and white boys
slept in rooms upstairs? I wonder if this
man, alone, on his way to see Viola, who
I think about now, is my angel.

A Winter Night

I watch his back
as he turns on the light.
His pajamas have a pattern
of colorful biplanes.
I cannot see him
as he climbs the counter.
I hear him open
the box and pour the cereal
into a bowl.
I see him go to the refrigerator
and take out the water.
I hear him pour it in a glass.
I hear him crunching,
but I cannot see him.
I listen to it from
the dining room.
I can see the refrigerator
and hear its motor.
I see the white stove
and white back door,
the black outside.
The 1999 calendar on the wall.
It is January and it is bedtime.
He is eight.
I am forty-five
and can still feel
him in my arms.
This is sentimental,
but I don't care.
I hear him take a drink.
He puts the dishes
in the sink
turns off the light

and goes upstairs.
He does not see me
watching him, but
he knows I am there
in his confident night.

LUCKY STRIKES

I used to smoke Lucky Strikes
because I liked the name and
the design on the pack and
the smell of the fresh tobacco.
I kept the pack in the refrigerator
and smoked about 2 or 3 a day
and 1 or 2 at night. I mean
there was no need to go crazy.
A pack lasted me about a week.
It cost 35 cents a pack
at the local smoke shop.
I smoked in the evening
on the porch. I was in college.
I knew I would quit after college
and I did a year or so after.
I was 22.
I haven't smoked since.
I'm 45 now.
I figure when the kids are grown,
I'll get back to it.
My wife won't mind.
A few cigarettes a day.
Maybe one.
One cigarette is enough,
outside at night.
There's no need to go crazy.

One was a ghost and some were themselves.
I was a hobo with burnt cork on my face
with tattered trousers and hat from
Goodwill I bought for twenty-five cents.
October air was still and cool and white.
The bus curved past potato fields, gray
shingled houses, ancient trees, young
forests and pick-up trucks. We sang
eighth grade songs and clowned
about the Halloween dance
with Sacred Hearts Academy
for dark-haired and red-haired girls.
Mr. Adams smoked Chesterfields
up front and combed his hair.
I wondered if the tall girl would be there.
She had to stoop over to dance with me.
I liked her pink smile and sleek arms
around me. She was in ninth grade
but I didn't care.
One was a cowboy and some were themselves.
All were jumpy and restless.
Seniors had whiskey in the back.
Seventh graders wriggled in front.
Sophomores stared with distracted expressions.
Adams loosened his tie,
pulled up his argyle socks.
We turned to Sag Harbor and up
to the academy by the water.
A skinny man with a goatee stood
in a tan raincoat, wind blowing some hair,
his shoulders up and tense.
"Quiet," said Adams, "That's John Steinbeck
on the corner."

Some of us looked and shook his hand;
most were too eager to meet girls.

Dan Sklar

Feet Feet

These feet are feet feet.
These knees are knees knees.
These ribs are ribs ribs
These shoulders are shoulders shoulders.
These lips are lips lips.
This nose is nose nose.
These eyes are eyes eyes.
This hair is hair hair.
This boy is boy boy.
This girl is girl girl.
These feet are feet feet.

WHAT IS IT ABOUT MOBY DICK?

I want to write poetry and my wife
wants me to paint the kitchen.
I want to have something to say like
"It's a *White Whale*, I say."
What did Mrs. Ahab nag him about?
"See someone, Ahab, you're obsessed!
See what you are doing to the children?
See how the house is falling apart!
See how the doorknob comes off!
See the water in the basement!
See how you clomp around all night!
See how I do not sleep, Ahab!
See how you dream about that silly
White Whale with the crazy name!
Moby Dick, Moby Dick, Moby Dick!
Everything is Moby Dick, Moby Dick."
My boys say, "Call me Ishmael"
with a conviction that stirs the
"Catskill eagle in *my* soul"
Ahab was a leader of men.
He knew why the men came.
He brought them to it.
One thing to do—one thing.
One promise—one oath.
My kids are spellbound
by Moby Dick, by Ahab,
by Queequeg, by the whalers,
by the bigness, awayness of it.
What is it about Moby Dick?
I'll write a play about it, I say
to my son, and he says:
"But your plays are funny.
There is nothing funny

Dan Sklar

about Moby Dick."
And everything is funny
about Moby Dick.
We all need a White Whale with
a crazy name in our lives because
it is a matter of Ahab degrees.

NATURE IS ITS OWN POEM

At the poetry reading

a man asked if the ocean

and woods inspired me.

I said they did not and that

ended the conversation.

Dan Sklar

Poetry Rewards and Honors and Literary Prizes

How can one have
distinct literary merit?
I don't have it,
distinct literary merit
that is. I mean,
that's my problem.
I ain't got it,
distinct literary merit
which is what
I do not have.
What I do have
is mediocre hack
literary merit, that's
what I have.
Any honors for that?
What I do have
is a kid that
plays the saxophone,
another kid that stands
on the table and sings,
and a wife that dances.

FISH

We took the fish to the backyard
to bury them.
We dug a hole with
a soup spoon I grabbed
from the kitchen.
He took it in stride
that the fish died.
After I covered them with earth
and patted it down
and he took three
stones and placed them
near them, I said,
"Should we say a few words?"
He held up
his hands and turned
his head toward the
house and said,
"No, Dad. Don't say
anything. Let's just go inside."

Dan Sklar

LAUGHING BUDDHA, VINCENT FERRINI

You are a wiry force of nature, Vincent,
From the ground of this Earth Star.
You filled my arms with your books
and my head with your Buddha eyes.
I hear the laugh, "ha" in Buddha,
and the bud of Buddha
that is the flower that is and was
and will be you the Laughing Buddha,
Wiry Buddha. In two minutes
with you, I learned how to write
the beauty of life, how to see
the beatifulness in the world,
in the eyes of the world,
the lightning flash of nowness
and thenness and all timeness.
What was it that drew me to Lynn
and Salem and Gloucester?
What is it in this rocky,
crooked, scattered northeast, factory,
beaches, mansions, three family houses,
tenements, development houses
wet night road towns that pulled me
with no job here? It was Denise
and her Italianness and her houses
filled with people. And it was your life
poems and life plays and you living
in your studio in the back room
theater of the world, on the stage,
behind the stage, in the wings,
in the audience, outside the theater
in the loneliness forever in the theater
Earth Star, making frames
and poems and plays

76

up on charges of tax evasion
up from General Electric nights
up from the shoe factory smoke
and into the marshes and Cape Anne
fishes mystery.
Sure when you cross the bridge
the light and the world changes.
The *Captain Courageousness* of it,
broken streets, ancient houses,
fish processing plants where you
cannot find a door or window,
and the boats on the docks
and in the watercolors from 1948.
You are the antipoet
because someone has to be
and poetry is life and the way to
write a poem is to love nature
and people and live in the world
and write everything at once
and mean everything at once.

Dan Sklar

One Day

When I drive Max to camp
or walk to town with Sam
I think of how it is temporary.
The tide is in, it is July
Denise's face is smooth
and wide. Her eyes are
calm and she is not worried.
I think of how in our house
there was a time we were
not there and there will be
a time we are not there but
in the dreams of my boys.
In my pocket are phrases
scribbled on scrap paper
what Sam said yesterday.
"Dream, dream, dream,
dream, dream, dream,
dream, dream, dream."
I have written to my friend
Russell whose daughter
fell out of a tree.
He used to climb trees.
What was I thinking
when I drove Max to camp?
It was something I wanted
to write about.
I was thinking about walking
with my sons, anyplace,
walking and how walking
someone will see us
from a bicycle or car
or walking and that will be all
of it. A father and his sons

walking in a small city
in New England by the ocean.
It will mean no more and no less
than that. This happiness
will be the dreams
of my boys grown up--
the happiness of a mother
and father and two sons
which was neither remarkable
nor new. It just was once.

March 30, 2000

Today I bought a bass and tom toms

and cymbal

Robin Hood Three-Speed Press

Titles:

Hack Writer

The Beautiful Trail

Jazz on Saturday, March 4, 2000

I put on Charlie Parker and oh, man! I know

what Kerouac meant about "Ornithology"

about anything Parker played and to have

played drums with Charlie Parker! I mean

there is nothing you can write or say about

Charlie Parker you just have to hear it.

I mean it gets into your blood the beat

and the swing the tight tightness as tight

as the skin of a snare drum but what I wanted

to write was that you have to listen to

Charlie Parker because someone has to. I had to

get back to playing the drums like when I was

eleven to songs like "I Cover the Waterfront"

and Parker records and then take it up again at

46 with my nine year old son Max on the alto

saxophone we bought November 22, 1999, 36

years after J.F.K was shot and it was the same

bright warm kind of day and I was nine when

it happened. Now Sammy, four years old,

sings. I mean I've got my own jazz band

and it is what I have always wanted.

Fifty-One Haiku

Car across the street
covered with snow. Think of her
alone in the house.

Friday icy night
kids spar in karate as
middle-aged dads watch.

Cannot explain how
much Max loves Chinese food. His face,
face, face, face shows.

Let's study haiku
in Japan, I say. Max says,
if Godzilla's there.

Bicycles and drums
and canoes and bicycles
and canoes and drums.

46 and I
have said everything there is
I am through talking.

When I turned forty-
six, I wanted to sit in
the sun all day long.

Lost piece of paper
with a great haiku on it.
Bullfrogs in the pond.

Cool June cloudy days

makes me think of childhood and
the sand in my shoes.

I had to call you
because your face and eyes are
like a great white cat.

Riding up to my
house and now leaning my bike
against the white fence.

Eating bananas
and swinging in the hammock,
Sammy and Dad too.

Statistics are more
important than stars and moons
It's a proven fact

When everyone is
sleeping, you must listen to
Thelonious Monk.

I watch Max smile
when he sees Buster Keaton's
name on the credits.

Two crows drink from a
puddle on the tennis court
near the factory.

Tree roots push through the
sidewalk concrete I like the
busted up cement.

Swings and jungle gyms
on a rocky hill school yard
where witches were hanged.

Under the shade of
a Maple tree listening
to Duke Ellington.

When I was young I
set out to write a novel.
It turned out haiku.

I want to kiss the
neck of a tall woman now.
This is forty-five.

On a professors
salary at a third-rate
college, I'm happy.

Listen to Ella
Fitzgerald from another
room. This happiness.

Denise sings Ella
"I'm Old Fashioned." Sam eats ice
cream. Max does homework.

Heavy leaves, no wind
Last day of May. I am home.
How long can it last?

Sears wants to sell me
life insurance. Life boils

to a mailing list.

You will grow old here,
My colleague tells me. And I
say it has happened.

One minute ago
I was a kid digging on
the beach. I watch mine.

It is Denise's
broad shoulders that I adore
to kiss and to kiss.

You've nothing better
to do than write haiku here?
Paint the kitchen now!

It dawned on me most
times no poem needs to be much
longer than haiku.

Trees in the distance
on a hill and think of her
pink arms, long fingers.

Li Po dropped his poems
in the river. He was a
vivid drunk. I'm next.

It is good to write
poems on the back of receipts
then throw them away.

Wind chimes, shadows of
leaves on a white fence, tall grass.
Sad for no reason

It's important to
read Damon Runyon now be—
cause someone has to.

A neighbor girl calls
Sam hears her & bolts for her.
"I want to see her."

Little girls sneak looks
at Max. He doesn't see it.
I see them watch him.

It is important
to see *Dodsworth* with Walter
Houston. You have to.

Sometimes I want to
walk far away like the old
Japanese poets.

Sam Says our house is
old and rusty. Max says he
never wants to leave.

Opera singing in
the house upstairs this July—
no one to hear it.

To write haiku and
to ride a horse on the beach-
this is a good life.

Dan Sklar

Max plays Mamillius
in *The Winter's Tale* with the
Rebel Shakespeare Co.

Riding a horse, time
does not matter with horses
walking the earth trails.

Lobster traps in weeds—
all these salty things—bird sings—
summer times in mind.

When you are in a
Shakespeare play you live Shakespeare—
a beautiful world.

A man smokes a big
cigar and watches the sea—
his children are grown.

The bottom of old
boats, dented, peeling, splintered—
with shadows of leaves.

There is nothing like
sitting in the shade reading
haiku—Sam comes soon.

How Sam loves French-fries—
wants to eat them every day—
ketchup and his face.

Pale July sky, beach—
long shadow of a scotch pine—

playground jammed with kids.

She runs the meeting
I watch her long fingers and
drink root beer and scotch.

Nine years old is Zen
is nine years old nuttiness.
Zen is nine years old.

Comes to my office
paces, looks around wants to
learn. I say don't want.

Jazz is in Max &
Max is in jazz & jazz is
in me and jazz is.

Dan Sklar

THE ESSENTIAL TOOL BOX

Sam, 3, plays with tools

from my tool box—pliers,

wrench, hammer,

vice-grips, assorted bolts

& nuts & brackets

& chain & unidentifiable

things thrown in

& saved for unknowable,

forgotten reasons.

He's working

on an imaginary project.

"I'm careful, Dad,"

he says to me & he is

even though I have not

said a word.

THIS SETTLES THE ABRAHAM & ISAAC & GOD THING

Abraham knew God was testing him

& knew God would stop him & knew

God knew he would not do it even if

he knew God would let him he knew

God knew he would not really do it.

Dan Sklar

THE KID

You can say anything you

like about Charlie Chaplin.

But the scene in *The Kid*

where Charlie fights officials

and the Kid fights too

to keep them from dragging

the Kid to an orphanage and

they put the Kid in the back

of the truck and the Kid is

crying and reaching for Charlie

and Charlie gets free, escapes

and runs on the rooftops

following the truck on the street

gets me every time.

How To Be Forty-six

Saturday, March 18, 2000
Denise is dancing today
Max and Sam are in their
pajamas playing together
in the living room,
imaginary stories
I am here trying to think
of things to write about
there is snow on the ground
I am trying to figure out
how to conduct myself
at 46 even though at every
age I have tried to figure out
how to act and many times
got it wrong and am feeling
like I am getting 46 wrong
I wonder how to get 46 right.
I have to be more patient
with Max and Sam and more
loving to Denise and warmer
to my colleagues and more
trusting. I mean I really have a
problem with trusting people.
I really believe some people
are out to get me. I am lucky I
land on my feet when I get
in trouble, probably because I
am popular with students and
the reason I am popular is
because they learn something
from me and because I teach
them the art of writing and am
honest with them and respect

93

them as individuals and do
not think of them as numbers
to be categorized, but after
two years one pretty much gets
what they can from a teacher.
I need new angles on life
and teaching and being a
husband and father and friend
and brother and son and jazz
drummer and playwright
and poet and writer and looker
at beautiful things and thinker
about beautiful things which
is what I want to do most
of the time is look at beautiful
things and think about beautiful
things and what I would like
to do is to take pictures of Max
and Sam and Denise next to
masterpieces and great and good
and even bad paintings
and sculptures in all the museums
in the world like I did with Max
at the Museum in Boston,
him at five next to Gauguin
Vincent van Gogh and Picasso
and Hopper and Pollock and
Birchfield paintings while Denise
was home after Sammy just born.
I have to cut out desire in the mind
mind desire, and have to be more
Zen about things and let people
be themselves and let people
think what they think because
they do anyway and I cannot
change other people, they do

what they do to survive I guess
just like me, but I can change
the way I act and think. Now I
think about the time I was skating
on Mill Pond in Port Washington
with my friend Eric Leifson,
and the ice broke and we fell in
up to our knees and went to a
house across the street and I
called my mother who came
and picked us up. I think that
of all the places I have lived I
like the name Port Washington
best for some reason and I imagine
and remember my childhood
as being like Tom Sawyer's.
I was not as wild as Huckleberry
Finn so I thought of myself as
Tom Sawyer in the woods
and on the beaches and riding
my bicycle to the candy store
or movies or grocery store
and the town docks where I
fished and used to catch huge
flounder and come home and play
the drums to the records
of Bobby Darin, Nat King Cole,
and The Beatles, and maybe
watch Laurel and Hardy
and Abbott and Costello movies
on TV and go to the movie theater
where I saw *Old Yeller* and
Journey to the Center of the Earth
and a crazy funny movie,
Dr. Strangelove. I liked to look
around Mercury's 5 and 10 Cents Store,

at the dusty toys and bags full of plastic
World War II army soldiers.
Sometimes I would be gone all day
on my bicycle. Childhood is such
a small part of our life in years,
but its impact is great on the rest of it.
When my parents got divorced
in 1964 and my mother moved
to York Avenue and 79th Street,
that summer I wondered Manhattan
and even went to the World's Fair by
myself. I think I like being alone
as long as there is plenty of life
going on around me the way it is now,
with Max and Sam playing together.
I cannot think of anything
better to write than that.

Godzilla An Epic Poem

I am writing an epic poem
about Godzilla because Godzilla
is important to me and to kids
and it strikes a sweet fear deep
in us and it is fake and real.
It is the people running.
A mother with a baby, school
children with rectangular backpacks—
their teacher hair messed,
panicked but controlled & clear
in her instructions, always last.
Godzilla is tortured. Godzilla is
tormented. Godzilla is complicated
Godzilla is angry. Godzilla is angry.
Godzilla is a teenager. I feel like
Godzilla sometimes. My wife says
my writing is a hobby. My sons want
me to play. They don't want
me to write. Max wants to talk
about Godzilla & Mothra & King Kong.
Godzilla always comes back—
he loses but comes back.

Dan Sklar

Old Men

Old men have

too many things

in their pockets

and eat cheese

sandwiches from

little wax paper

sandwich bags

and remember

playing baseball,

the sunny field,

and realize they

have always been

ready to die.

(Three Found Poems from *Public Speaking Principles and Practice*)

TYPES OF AUDIENCES: CONCERTED GROUP

Top,
the military
unit responds
immediately
to a command
given by officer
in charge.

Bottom,
modern dance
class executes
movements when
instructor gives
command.

THE TIMES AND PLACES MEN SPEAK ARE LEGION

The pictures
on the facing
page show
Senator Arthur
Vandenberg
and a minister
and a laborer.

WENDELL WILLKIE

The effective speaker shows
his alertness by his posture.

In the presidential campaign

of 1940, Wendell Willkie,

Republican nominee, won
the admiration of millions

of Americans by his
directness and enthusiasm.

Why?

There is something sad

about walking in on some

old professor eating a ham

sandwich on white bread

in his office at 11:00 AM.

Dan Sklar

Buster Keaton Running

I should have gone into the hat or cigar business.
My son Maxfield says he will be a professor of comedy.
He says his favorite color is all the colors in the world;
that his favorite animal is squids, but he likes all
animals. He says he wishes he was Buster Keaton
climbing all over the General. I have been thinking
about Buster Keaton so I read a book about him
Why Buster Keaton? What is it about him that
I think about him? When he was forty they said he
was through but he didn't think so.
He did not stop working. He smoked
three to four packs of cigarettes a day.
He drank and played solitaire. He played bridge.
He watched TV. He went to Europe.
He was married three times.
His third wife was twenty-one when he was forty-five.
He drove a Cadillac.
He makes me laugh and he is tragic.
Sam, one, laughs when he sees Buster.
Max, six, runs like Buster.
I read about his life and think
I understand what he went through,
though I am not a genius at anything.
Buster Keaton was in vaudeville
when he was a kid.
He got into movies when he met Roscoe Arbuckle
on the street in New York, by chance.
What does it all mean? Somehow Buster gets me
thinking about my kids, Samuel and Maxfield,
what they will do,
what they will be.
What act
can I
teach them?

Buster Keaton

Buster Keaton, what would you do with a computer?

It would get you and you would fight it with your

stone face, your straight face. You would be eaten

by it because that is what it does. It says write in

me and do it now and do it quickly too and do not

think because it will do the thinking for you and

it will spell wrong for you and keep you from

sleeping because of how it happened so fast

and you could not bring it back once it went out

and one mistake will do you in, one mistake

because you could not think straight so in

your mind you realize you could lose it all

like Buster Keaton lost it all, but Buster Keaton

was Buster Keaton and I am no Buster Keaton.

There are no B pictures for me or Europe or

Mexico or a *General* or *Seven Chances*.

A Paranoid Middle-aged Professor

Here are some notes on
the new creative writing
major at the college
where I work and
which probably has come
about as a result of the
Peter principle because
I am good when
I am teaching people
who are not interested
in learning how to write
with some sort of
truth and expression so
they do but when it comes
to students who want to be
writers and happen to be
good at it I as a teacher
have something missing
because it is really weird
actually that my boss, and
I don't mean to be a wise
guy even though that is
what I am, says that he
is invested in this and
wants to ensure that it
will work and I am just
a guy who is a pretty okay
writer but am basically
a hack who gets a few
laughs from the students
and knows a few of the
writing terms and maybe
can convey them to the

students sometimes but
really I am just a house
painter who got lucky
with a couple of poems
I wrote for the hell of it
and now some people call
me a poet when I am not
a poet or am no more of
a poet anymore than any
sensitive person who happens
to look at the world and love
it and write about it in
any kind of genuine way
when the truth is after teaching
for about twenty years I am
somewhat through with it
because I have said all that
I have to say about it even
though I have to keep saying
it again to new students and
see these new Profs. younger
then me who call themselves
poets because one went to
Radcliff and has received a
grant for thirty-five thousand
dollars to write poems for a
year and that is all just to write
poems for a year and I mean
no one is giving me thirty-five
cents to do anything and another
poet had two poems in *Poetry
Magazine* the magazine that
wouldn't publish my poems in
a million years for Christ sake's
and besides half of the poems
in *Poetry Magazine* have no

guts and the other half are too
goddamn crafted only other
poets and educated institutional
administrators who went to Barnard
and wanted to be poets give a damn
about them and I get these memos
from my boss saying what about
this person or that person who go
around saying we're poets for
teaching other sections of my
classes and the truth is they want
my job and this is the place I find
myself in at this nervous
breakdown moment at forty-six
years old in my life when I am
paranoid and loaded with
an incredible amount of low
self-esteem and have been making
rambling meaningless speeches
where I recite haiku which I write
and my colleague says my haiku
are chopped liver compared to
Robert Haas' haiku he is right and
tells me I better be careful or else I
will get old at this college and I tell
him it has happened and I have
because 1200 people do not care
about haiku as they are looking at
a college for their kid and here is
this crazy nut faculty member
telling bad Babe Ruth stories
I mean I feel like everyone is
out to get me and I don't want
anyone invested in anything
I do or needing to ensure
anything where I am involved.

Sonnet to Duse

What is it about Eleonora Duse?
I look at her photograph and read
books about her and then give the
books away and do not want them
again and there can be no play
about her because she has to be
in my troubled thoughts and one
cannot act a sunbeam deep in the
woods or a moonbeam on a quiet
road. Eleonora Duse is the actor's
patron saint in her humanness
and besides, it is the image and
idea and eyes and lips of her
that means anything in the end.

Dan Sklar

Zen

This

is

This

is

This

Is

This

Is

This

is

The

way

The

way

It

is

It

is

It

is

It

is

Dan Sklar

No Time Even to Write This Crummy Poem

It is not funny
anymore the fact
that I have
nothing to write
and the fact that
I have started
a play but it sits
there and goes
nowhere while
I have reached
the point at
which I do not
have time at all
to do anything
even though you
say I do I mean
there isn't even
time to sit and
smoke a cigar
and listen to jazz
and think about
nothing except
the fact that
in Ushuaia
which is a port
in Tierra del Fuego
the people raise
sheep and go
fishing at least
according to
my kid's atlas
they do so I
think I want

to go there
to be one
of the people
who raises
sheep and
goes fishing.

Anger

My
wife
says
I
am
an
angry
person
but
my
poems
are
beautiful.
This
is
because
life
and
the
world
is
bigger
than
my
anger
at
it.

Night Rain Fire Pond Beat

We played conga drums
did not stop rained they
put up tarps
built a fire played
conga drums guitars read
plays poems smoked
cigarettes drank rain
came let up came again
pond reflected fire
us wind blew smoke
groups of people came
listened danced moved
on in rain we could see
patches of forests boulders
shiny in rain night
brick buildings loaded
with florescent lights
chalk boards
People looked out library
windows our drums
flew across campus
beat of us who we are
March Thursday night I
smoked cigars
played congas
hat pulled over eyes.
I was 46
they were 19
At home my
wife kids slept
rain on Sam's tricycle
on Max's baseball
What it means is

Dan Sklar

night fire
guitars drums
nineteen years olds
forty-six year old
drums pond chalk boards
empty classrooms
poems plays
one rainy
March night of it
drumming the
one rainy beat night of us

Paddle Slowly

You suddenly
find yourself
reading back
issues of
Wooden Canoe
and studying
the pictures
of people at
the canoe
building events
they hold.
The articles
are written
in correct
English.
There is no
hurry in
Wooden Canoe
like there is no
hurry in
a canoe.

Paper

I was thinking about scrap paper and how I like all kinds of paper Composition Notebooks, loose-leaf paper, writing tablets, paper with blue lines, red margins, no lines, crumpled paper, ripped paper, paper torn out of notebooks, old journal paper, scratch pad paper, you name it. I like tearing open envelopes and reading the paper, folding the paper, putting the paper somewhere else. I like writing anything on paper. That's why I like teaching English because of all the paper work. Maybe I should have gone into the paper business? Actually, I almost went into the box making business in North Carolina by marrying my college girlfriend whose father was a box manufacturer and I was going to learn the business. She already had a little house on a woodsy street, but she did not love how I wanted to write plays and she did not think I had the talent really, and even if I did, she wanted a professional type money making man and besides that she was still stuck on her old boyfriend and said he was a better lover than me. She had a big dopey silver Ford Mustang Mach something or other. (A little red horse lit up on the dashboard when you put the brights on.) Who cares? It was 1974. I was 21. I took a train from Manhattan to get engaged in North Carolina. I met five SCUBA divers on their way to Florida. They were drinking whiskey, playing poker, and looking at naked women in a magazine. I told them I was an English Professor at Southampton College, what a lie. It did not matter to them. In my subconscious this was my desire. When the train pulled into Raleigh I was downright drunk and she knew it and it gave her an excuse to be displeased with me. I passed out for a moment-face first into eggplant Parmesan in the romantic side street, narrow Italian Restaurant. I remember liking the feel of the warm eggplant on my face. The next day her father showed me around the box factory. Grim workers in gray polyester uniforms, concrete floor, cinder block walls, no windows-it was built that way.

Conveyor belt and cutting, folding, packing, printing, whirring machines and boxes rolling off into piles and stacks in neat brown practical, functional, usefulness. His office was stark. I'm talking austere, not a picture of a wife or kid or dog or anything. Steel gray office supplies store furniture, florescent lights, no windows, seriously, no windows. I cannot recall anything he ever said to me. That night he threw us an engagement party in a downtown hotel. The shrimp cocktails were still a bit frozen and the stuffed fish type dish tasted like the freezer. He gave me the least expensive Seiko wristwatch, which stopped a month later. There was a big cake with creepy blue icing and in white letters said "Debbie and Danny". No one's heart was in this thing. After bad sex and no sleep that night I walked to the nearby shopping center and watched the fog in the lights. I called my mother from a phone booth to tell her I was calling it off. No one was heart broken. (The relationship never really worked since the time she jammed an antique cup and saucer in her purse and swiped it from a fancy restaurant in Boulder, Colorado.) I took the afternoon train to Manhattan thinking of paper. Looking at blank paper in an Original Big Chief Writing Tablet and thinking of white paper. On her way to the Regency Bridge Club my mother asked me what I was going to do now that the box factory thing was through. "I don't know," I said, but I was thinking about something to do with paper and it suddenly occurred to me. It dawned on me. This was my destiny—paper, loaded with words!

Dan Sklar

March Winds

I fought the wind as a boy
delivering the *Long Island Press*
to development houses.
Solid Robin Hood three-speed
and me with crew cut pushing
through March winds, folding
papers and placing them in
mailboxes or screen doors of
little houses with patchy lawns,
each had its warm sour smell.
Wind pulled veins across the bay
where I stopped to have a Milky Way—
Fingers red and cold, wind
whizzing over my ears.
I waved to kids I recognized from
school but didn't know.
Delivered to the Republican Club,
puffy men in tight suits sat at
the bar. I'd grab a handful of
peanuts, hop on my bike and race
up the pebbly driveway and
line of tall pine trees to tiny
houses where old men cooked suppers
at four in the afternoon.
O, the March wind stung my face.
The sun went down around six-thirty
when I put my bike in the garage.
Dinner smelled great and my dog,
Happy, jumped all over me.
I put hot water on my fingers
and face.
The lights sparkled like candles
and dinner was beef stew

and apple pie with ice cream.
My old paper route.
What a route! What a life!

My Poetry

My poetry will never win a contest.
It will not get into magazines like *Poetry*
or get me a big fat grant I would use
to pay for private school for my kids
or to buy another car so I would
not have to ride my bicycle to work
in the rain.
It will not get me into Yaddo
or some artists retreat. I'd miss
my sons, Max and Sam, too much.
I wouldn't want to give up their
great interruptions, smiling like mad,
sneaking in crazy where I work.
I have lost more insights and lines
because I let them go and lost them
to be with my kids—simple as that.
I'll never have a book published
because when I dig down deep
I am happy.
I love my wife and dream about her.
I like teaching and this middle-class life.
That's about the extent of my theme.
I'll probably never afford a sailboat
or car with less than 113,000 miles on it.
Some days I do not give a damn about poetry
and I just want to make money.
I want to clear out all the books
and papers from my office, get rid
of the computer the school issued.
The Royal manual is still on my desk.
I put new ribbons on the old spools.
I have nothing against computers.
I prefer the trees and rocks and sky.

RAIN

Sometimes it is good

to stay in a motel

March in the rain

by the ocean

raining

in a town where

most everything is shut

down and it is good

to be in this motel

you stayed in before

when you were

not alone

and could not

watch rain.

Dan Sklar

Baseball Is

My father handing cash to the old ushers
at Yankee Stadium for better seats,
my old four fingered Stan Musial glove.
Now I have a Whitey Ford mitt,
but you know it doesn't matter.
I used to flip cards in the schoolyard
Plenty of Mickey Mantles—
Elston Howards—
the names to me then like Greek Gods.
Studying the cards, chewing the gum,
loving the uniforms;
Pretending to be a play by play
radio broadcaster on reel to reel.
Now I ignore the players
and teams and don't care about
the salaries and gossip and standings
and records and statistics.
I care about you know what to expect
and what not to expect.
It is the theater—and drama and sky
of the game that is everything.
And what it is is me and my sons
just like me and my dad
in the theater of it—
having catches in the backyard
with our mitts with some ball player's
name wearing off.

The Paperboy

When I was twelve and wanted to be alone, I used to deliver the Long Island Press after school and Saturdays and Sunday mornings. The stack of papers would be on the stoop near the front door when I got home. I'd untie the string and spilt the stack in two to put them in the baskets over the back fender of my red Robin Hood three-speed bicycle. Sometimes I went into the house before going on the route, but mostly I just took off as soon as I was ready. I had the route for a couple of years. I would get off my bicycle at the different houses, pull a paper from the basket, fold it and place it in the screen doors or mailboxes. I was in no hurry.

Each house had its own warm sour smell. There was a cool musty smell like wet chalk in the Republican Club where I also delivered. The bar was dark, but the bottles and mirror and glasses glistened. There was usually a man wearing a hat at the bar and dressed in a suite and tie. The bartender never looked at me, even when I was collecting. I left the paper on the bar and sometimes grabbed a handful of peanuts and ate them as I rode my bicycle up the gray gravel and line of tall pine trees.

I delivered to the tiny one-bedroom development houses. I knew some of the kids who lived in that neighborhood. There was one girl who was also in my class. Her name was Kathy McKenna. She had long red hair and a red smile and she was wide though not fat and she said she was my girlfriend. I didn't know where she got that idea and whenever she said it, I said nothing because I didn't know what she was talking about. I had another friend, Tom Whalen, from one of those houses. His father was a handyman for the town. He ate beef and noodles every night and his wife complained about it, but that was what he wanted so that was what she cooked. She smiled a lot and was glad the boy was my friend. She always seemed to stare at me, like she was trying to figure something out about me. One time she asked me if I was going to go to college. I said I was and she said you see that Tom, Danny's going to college! The boy was always asking me if I was Irish. He wanted me to be an Irish Catholic like him.

As I rode on my paper route I used to wave to kids I knew from school and some kids I just recognized. There were some tough Italian kids who used to holler out, "There goes Danny with the bagaloon pants." Tight pants were in fashion. I wore old khaki trousers and a blue button-down shirt my mother bought from Brooks Brothers in New York.

We lived in Blue Point, but used to go to the city every few months to go shopping or to a museum or sometimes to see a show. When my parents got divorced and before my mother remarried, we moved from Port Washington to 79th Street at York Avenue. She took me to see the *Mikado*. I sat on the top of the seat and ate a big doughy salty pretzel with an orange drink. The drink felt good in my mouth after the bite of the salt. My mother and I laughed at the songs and jokes in the show. We'd go out after the shows to restaurants like Longchamps where they had white table clothes and French food. I would have a hamburger and she would have something French and a couple of whiskey sour drinks. She was forty and divorced and very sad and lonely.

I was eleven that summer and spent much of the time playing my drums to Beatle records in my room and going places by myself in New York. The city was pretty safe in those days, 1964. Sometimes I'd spend all day at the Museum of Natural History. I loved the displays of animals in their natural habitat and wanted to be up there in the cold arctic where there was nothing but ice and sky and no cars or people. I'd imagine the squid and whale fighting in the depths of the ocean and I would sit under the blue whale contemplating its enormity. And I was spellbound in the African tribes' section, the masks and shields and drums and jungleness of it. I used to walk over to Central Park and watch people I didn't know play baseball and then I'd walk through the Central Park Zoo. I didn't go in because the cages with nervous monkeys and lions and animals made me feel lonelier. I went to the movies in the morning sometimes, and wanted to see *A Hard Days Night* which had just come out. It was a theater on Second Avenue and I was used to paying 25 cents a ticket, suburb prices. When the lady said it was 60 cents I was dumbfounded. She was a very thin woman with a thin wrinkly face and her gray curls were high on her head. She wore thick glasses and had on a pale blue sweater. I told her all I had was thirty-five cents. That didn't matter she said, it cost sixty cents. I stepped away from the window and looked at the poster of the Beatles jumping in the air with wild, happy expressions.

I went around the corner and sat on a stoop and counted my change again. I could barely see the coins as my eyes filled and I felt the silent thunder build in my head and my mouth filled with saliva. My parents were divorced and I couldn't see *A Hard Days Night* and I was crying about all of it at once. I felt a hand on my shoulder and looked up at the thin woman's glasses. She told me to come with her and she led me to a side entrance of the theater. I managed to say that I had thirty-five cents. She took the money and hurried me in. The theater was cool and dark. I liked how Ringo was lonely and how he and I both played the drums. I watched the movie twice.

Sometimes riding my bicycle I'd look down at the pavement and think about that summer. That summer I let myself get lost in the Metropolitan Museum of Art and let the knights' armor take me to the middle-ages and the Egyptian mummies and hieroglyphs take me to Thebes and the time I took the subway to the World's Fair and went on the gondola and the monorail and into the Triumph of Man pavilion where they gave out little red records with a grave announcer highlighting the history of humankind and dramatic symphony music in the background. I loved to listen to that record at home and was intrigued with the cave men and the city of Ur and Mesopotamia. And I'd listen to "Does Your Chewing Gum Lose its Flavor on the Bedpost Over Night," and "Big John," and "Goldfinger." It was a good and lonely summer. But now my mother was remarried and here we were living in Blue Point and I was delivering newspapers. I was happy.

There was this one girl in another class at school, but the same grade as me, who lived in a big old house on the Great South Bay. I used to see her in school and playing on the beach or in front of her house. Emily Miller had tight curly hair parted to the skin on one side of her head. I liked the lines on her long neck and her thick lips. She had three sisters and two brothers. The front door of her house was always open because her brothers and sisters and their friends were constantly running in and out. The floors were painted wood but the paint had worn off where most of the walking was done. There wasn't much on the walls either, just a cheap tapestry of John F. Kennedy with the White House in the background. The furniture was big and dark and oak. I liked Emily. I liked talking to her. I pulled my bicycle over to where she was playing and said hi to her.

"You have a big family," I said.

"I know," she said.

"I have two older brothers."

"Oh. They in college?"

"Yes."

"Oh."

"There are some horseshoe crabs on the beach."

"Man of war jellyfish out there too. You have to look out."

"My brother shot a seagull out of the sky. I wish he didn't."

"Want to come to my house?"

"I have to deliver these papers," I said, glad I had something important to do even though I did want to go to her house.

"Sometime."

"Sometime. Bye, Emily."

"Bye, Danny."

I got back on my bicycle and waved as I peddled standing up.

Across the street from my house was this tiny house where an old man lived. He was a thick bald man who moved slowly through the one room house and he cooked his supper of boiled hot dogs at four in the afternoon. The place always smelled like warm frankfurters. I delivered to his house first and collected from his house last. One time he invited me to step inside while he found his change

"You'd rather be playing baseball, right? And here you are delivering papers every afternoon. I bet you play football in the fall and baseball in the spring and summer, I bet."

"Yes," I said trying not to breathe the hot stale air. I wanted to run out of there. The truth was I had little interest in playing ball. I mean it was fun when I did and I liked it, but all that winning and losing didn't mean anything to me-it didn't seem very important. I said nothing more about it and when he talked about sports teams I didn't say anything because I didn't know anything about it.

One time he gave me a quarter as a tip. Usually people gave me a nickel or a dime. He seemed very pleased with himself when he gave me the quarter and I thanked him. I figured since we never found anything in common that we could talk about, giving me the big tip made him feel that somehow we connected.

At one house there was a man with bowlegs—I mean they really made a circle. Louis Armstrong was always blasting on the stereo and I often listened for awhile at the door. He played "Mack the Knife," a lot. When I was collecting, I could hear him struggle off the couch and work his way to the door. He had no teeth and white hair plastered down on his head. He wore plaid shirts and blue jeans. He didn't really look at me. He paid me and took his paper and went back to the couch and Louis Armstrong. I watched his bowlegs as he walked.

One Friday when I was collecting, his wife came to the door. There was no Satchmo playing. The wife looked awfully down and waited as if she wanted me to say something.

"What's the matter, Mrs. Bronkwell?"

"Al died," she said as if she really wanted to tell someone and I was the only one around.

"I'm sorry."

"Me too."

We didn't say anything more. We just stood there, she in the doorway and me on the stoop holding the paper. I didn't remind her I was collecting. I didn't know what to do. After what seemed like a long time. I handed her the paper. She took it and thanked me, but stayed right there as if we were having a conversation.

"He liked Louis Armstrong," I said.

"He did," she said and smiled and turned from me and closed the door.

There was a kid who sat behind me in class and he was blind with some fingers gone. He was a quiet kid named Adrian and he was a whiz at math and knew the answers to history and geography questions. He always said hello to me and I always said hi. What happened was he was playing with fireworks on Blue Point beach one July fourth and it blew some of his fingers off and blinded him. One time he tapped me on the shoulder after recess while we were waiting for the teacher to come back. He whispered to me that the packet was wrapped in paper with patterns of roses and leaves and that the instructions, which he read, stated to light the fuse and get away. He said he lit the fuse but it exploded before he could get away-I mean it blew up right away. He whispered the whole story to me and said he wasn't the kind of kid who played with fireworks, that was the first time and he didn't even know why he was doing it. Maybe it was because he was with a bunch of other kids-he didn't know. He said he just remembered the flash and the paper with roses and leaves on it. He was still holding some of the paper it was wrapped in and he could feel it wet with blood.

I used to see him sitting on his porch as I rode by on my paper route. Sometimes I said Hi, Adrian, and he said hi, Danny, and that was all. His face pointed up to the sky when he heard me. Sometimes his mother was out there sitting with him. They both had black hair and white skin. Every time I saw him I thought about his story and the paper with roses and leaves.

I would run and jump on my bicycle and really get up some speed after delivering to a house. I could usually ride faster than the dogs that chased me a few houses past their property. They would stop, still barking, and then head back, taking one more look at me while I took a last look back at them and they would bark a few more times as if to say, and don't come back. One time a collie chased me and managed to hook his white teeth into the cuffs of my trousers and then the teeth punctured the skin on my ankle. I felt the sharpness go up my leg. I shook him off and kicked him and he kept barking but I left him behind.

I pulled to the curb and dropped off my bike to see the damage. The blood soaked my sock. I peeled it down and looked at the two cuts the shape of a dog's teeth. I could walk on it so I got back on the bike and slowly continued the paper route and when I was done, went home.

I was alone. I put my foot in the sink and ran cold water on it. The bleeding was done. I put iodine on it and dried it and put Band-Aids on it. It was dusk and I did not turn any lights on in the house. I sat in the den in the dark, convinced the dog had rabies and that I would get ten shots in my stomach and I would die. I was glad.

I knew whose dog it was because I used to deliver the Press to them until they canceled. I called information to get the telephone number and then I dialed it. There was no answer. I was alone in the dark. I felt tragic and liked it. I never told anyone about it and the bite healed and nothing happened and that is all I remember about it.

By the time the sun was going down I was heading home. Sometimes I would stop by the beach and look at the water and the island across the bay. I don't know what I was thinking, but I know I liked the wind in my face and how the wind made veins and ripples in the water and the small waves on the beach and the sand. Sometimes I would have a Milky Way candy bar while I listened to the water. I liked the chocolate mixed with the salt air in my mouth. Sometimes I would think about the kids I knew and school and my bicycle and how my mother was happy now.

Scotch and Love and Adultery

"I can see a boat supply store, a brake and clutch shop, a run-down Victorian house apartment house, Al's Bait and Tackle, a place called Lounge with two neon martini glasses, a shack covered with red, blue, green, white, and yellow buoys, and a stack of lobster traps in front. There are some trees with their roots busting up the sidewalk cement, a variety store, a fire hydrant, the sky, cars parked and cars going north and south, weeds, oil tanks, some of the harbor. There's a rusty Datsun parking. Some of the seat belt is hanging out of the door. There's a woman in the car. She's looking at her face in the mirror. She's combing her hair. She's putting on lipstick. She's getting out of the car and coming this way. She has broad shoulders and a thin waist, too much lipstick, but that's okay, blonde, ponytail, bangs, small mouth, small breasts, long legs—good. She has a black purse over her shoulder, a sleeveless white blouse. No smile, long strides, nervous. She's heading for this building. She's coming in. She's coming up the stairs."

The man takes a deep breath. After a moment there is a knock on the door. The man looks at the door and then opens it. The woman doesn't come in right away. They look at each other for a moment.

"I'm here about this ad. I read it in the paper. The newspaper help wanted section. My name is Leisel Angstrom. I graduated in May. I have a five-year-old kid and I need a job and this sounded like something. I majored in liberal arts because—well just because. May I come in?"

"Yes."

"What's the job, exactly? My boy is with my mother. I don't have a husband because I don't. You see, I have to be up front with you right away because I have this kid, Carson, and there's no time to beat around the bush about anything. What's the job?"

"I don't know."

"Did you write the ad? Am I in the right place?

132

"Yes."

"I'm a bit confused."

"Why?"

"Look. Good-bye."

"Wait."

"Is this a gag or something weird?"

"No."

"I told you I don't have time. The ad was good. I want to get in on a business. That's what I want. What's the business?"

"I told you, I don't know yet."

"I'm through talking. I'm leaving."

"Listen. This is on the level. I've been looking for you. I don't mean anything crazy by all this. I really don't. I think I knew it when I first saw you."

"I have a five year old son. He is the most important thing to me. I live with my mother. She is the next most important thing to me. I answered your ad because I don't want to get into some corporate-type management training thing because I don't want to have meetings and plan strategies and write memos and get memos and tell people what to do and be told what to do or sell something people don't really need and never see my kid because I'm working all the time. Your ad was good. I want to get in on something right at the beginning because this is a beginning for me. This is my college diploma."

"Oh."

"You see, I've been to college. I have a BA in liberal studies with a focus in creative writing, because—well just because; and for me because is a good enough reason for anything. What will be my duties and tasks in this business?"

"You will decide that."

"When do I start?"

"You started."

"What's the salary? Benefits?"

"What do you want them to be?"

"You don't know much do you. And you don't say much either."

"What do you want?"

"You mean, how much money? What kind of benefits?"

"Yes."

"You know, this is getting a bit too weird for me. I got a kid, a mother, loans to pay. I'm really not interested in some guy's nervous breakdown mid-life crisis."

"Who said anything about a nervous breakdown?"

"You know something. I hate this cryptic crap. I want you to come clean—now."

"This is an empty office. Two empty rooms. The sun comes in certain times of the day whether anyone is here or not. It moves over the floor, the door, the wall, the ceiling, and disappears. You want some vanilla soda?"

"What?"

"Vanilla soda?

"Yes."

"They have some in that variety store down the street. Here. Get us a few bottles."

"Excuse me?"

"Please."

"Thank you."

"You're welcome."

"What the heck. But then I have to get going. Really."

"Take this."

She walks out.

"I hear her on the stairs. There she is on the sidewalk. She looks both ways before crossing the street. Some cars slow down. A man looks at her. She looks good. Long legs. She's going into the variety store. This is good. I have an empty office and a beautiful girl getting me vanilla soda. It's Tuesday morning. This is what I've wanted all the time, a cold vanilla soda, and an empty office, sun coming in a window, a woman. She's coming back. She is carrying a paper bag. She looks both ways. She's crossing the street. Guys slow down to look at her. She's coming into the building."

"Here's your soda."

"Thanks."

"You're welcome."

They each open a bottle.

"So, what's the deal?"

"You tell me."

"Got a typewriter? It seems to me a business ought to have a typewriter."

"No."

"Computer?"

"No."

"Paper?"

"No."

"Pencil?"

"No."

"What do you have?"

"Nothing."

"You know I did get something really good out of going to college; that is I keep a journal. I mean I use a journal and I have a pen. I'll take a letter. Let's write a letter to someone to kickoff this business. You can try me out and I can try you out—so to speak. I love to write things like, *To Whom it May Concern.*"

"I don't want to write a letter."

"How about a thank you note. Someone could always be thanked for something."

"No."

"A business has to conduct correspondence. You said this was a business. I'm going along with it. You ought to too. What exactly is on your mind?"

"Not a thing."

"Not a thing? Nothing? You mind if I write that?

"Go ahead."

"Now we're getting someplace. Go ahead is a positive thing to say. It moves us forward. I think we're on to something here. I will write things in this journal. I will write everything we have done and said so far. Is that all right with you?"

135

"It is."

"Very good. And I will write about something that I just remembered. I remember I used to dig for clams on the beach when I was a kid. I can feel the sun on my neck and my hands in the cool sand and feel that living thing holding on without a chance. I like the sound of the word oyster. I'll write that too. By the way, am I on a pay roll?"

"Yes."

"Will I like it?"

"Yes."

"Do I get business cards?"

"Do you want business cards?"

"I do."

"Get them."

"I want them to read, Leisel Angstrom, nothing else. Leisel Angstrom is enough."

"Good."

"May I go now?"

"Do you have to go?"

"Not really."

"Then stay. This is good."

"Where do you live?"

"Look, I don't want to…. In North Bridge."

"May I write that?"

"Yes."

"Where are you from?"

"New York."

"New York. Very good. It is excellent to be someone from New York. It makes you automatically interesting and important and you are living up to those characteristics. Very good. I am writing all of this in this journal and I will bring a new notebook for the business tomorrow. I'll write things in it. I am starting today. This is a good job so far."

"The soda is good. It's cold. It's sweet. I like it."

"Me too. I took a creative writing course in college where all we did was write in a journal. That was it. I'm beginning to like this job."

"I am too."

"But how can we make money? Are you independently wealthy?"

"I am."

"Ah ha! So that's it. I knew it. I could tell. You married? Divorced? Kids?"

"Yes."

"What did you do before this empty office?

"I like how this is an empty office. I'm thinking of keeping it empty."

"Why?"

"Because I don't want any file cabinets or telephones or anything."

"You don't?"

"Just the sun coming in that window, moving in shapes across the floor, on the wall, the door, the ceiling. Just me here and then just you and me."

"I'm writing what you say, you know."

"Right now, at this moment, there are file cabinets filled with folders with papers that have names and lies and truths about people in organizations and on computer files too.

There is a man in his thirties with two kids, somewhere right now, sitting in an office and another man is firing the man in his thirties. He is being fired because that particular organization doesn't have the money to pay him anymore. Some budget has been cut. They call it laid off, but he's been fired.

"Another man, sixty, a painter and teacher is not hired full-time by a college even though he desperately needs to be, but his credentials aren't right. The fact that he is a good teacher and artist and human being doesn't matter.

"Here, no one gets fired. No records are kept. It is a place to go to work when you get up in the morning and to feel good and right about it. You work here and I work here. Sometime we will go somewhere for a business meeting and make decisions and write a mission statement based on our philosophy of life and some policies and then tear it all up and start over. It will be good."

"Philosophy…good…yes.   I   will   wear   something businesslike yet feminine. It will be a dark and cool restaurant. I am writing what I say too, you know. This is a journal of business in an empty office. We can have a five year plan too."

"Right now a tall blonde woman has stepped into the office of a middle-aged man. She is a manager in an organization. They have been attracted to each other for two years. She closes the door. 'You said you have Scotch,' she says to the man. It is a hot July afternoon. 'I do,' he says to her. 'I want a drink. I just had to tell a guy he didn't get a job he's been vying for, and that he is through altogether—that an outsider got it. It wasn't easy,' she says.

"He takes a bottle and two glasses from the bottom drawer of his desk. The bottle is next to his shoe polish. He pours her a drink and one for himself. She drinks it—has another. In no time they are kissing. She had just gotten married in June. She had wondered why the man she was now kissing hadn't come to the wedding to take her away. He loves his wife and kids and the tall blonde too. It is going to be a mess. He knew he shouldn't stay in his office so much. It is scotch and love and adultery."

"Yes, scotch and love and adultery."

"I like sitting on the floor."

"Me too."

"Here is a key to the office."

"Thank you."

"Are you done for the day?"

"Yes. I have a son and mother at home. I didn't know I would start right away. What time tomorrow?"

"Anytime you want."

"When will you be here?"

"In the morning."

"I'll take my son to school, then come right over."

"Okay."

"Well, I think we got a lot accomplished. This is a good business. What I'll do is, I'll go over these things tonight and copy them into a business journal. How's that? Is that all right?"

"Yes, it is."

"Anything else?"

"No. Anything else for me?"

"No. So long."

"Bye."

"See you in the morning. You know, I'm worried about you."

"Don't worry."

"You'll need my social security number."

"I'll pay you in cash."

"But taxes and..."

"Never mind that."

"You know I have a kid and I need health insurance and..."

"I'll pay for it."

"I want a pension and my kid will go to college. I have to think of the future. I mean what if this business fails. I've got a kid to think about."

"Write all of that."

"I will. You know, you are a very poetical type person and all, but I've got loans and bills and a jalopy and I want to meet someone. I mean, I had this kid when I was eighteen. I wasn't going to marry his father—he was just a kid. I mean, how can I meet someone in this empty office?"

"Write it. You were through for the day. This is good overtime for you. Write it. Write everything we do. You have good questions. Questions are good business. Another soda?"

"No, thank you. I've got my work cut out for me tonight. I have to get another notebook and copy all this."

"Take this."

"What is it?"

139

"Your first days pay. Buy the notebook and the pen out of it."

"It's three hundred dollars."

"I know."

"But…"

"You worked hard"

"Not that hard."

"You wrote good things."

"Thank you."

"Good night, Leisel."

"Good night."

She goes out the door and he closes it and walks over to the window.

"She's going across the street to the car. She looks confused and delighted. She's smiling. She's getting into the car. The seat belt hangs from the door. She starts the car. Blue smoke pours out of the exhaust pipe. She's driving away. The afternoon sun is on the ceiling. The sun is going behind Al's Bait and Tackle shop. This soda is good."

Siberian Women

and the **Red Moon**

A Play by **Dan Sklar**

CHARACTERS

VALERIE L. VALENTINO *A Playwright*

COREY CAIN *Professor*

WALTER MARCH *Professor*

MRS. EILEEN LINCOLN *Patron*

HAZEL LINCOLN *Eileen's daughter*

ADELE LINCOLN *Eileen's daughter*

DIMITRY *Businessman*

MARCELLO *Thug*

RUPERT WILLIAMS *Minstrel*

MAURA OLSON *Innkeeper*

MELODY PLACE *Prostitute*

IVAN *Anna's boyfriend*

NATASHA *Ivan's girlfriend*

VIOLET CHIMES *Short-order cook*

LENNY *Thug*

ANNA *Dancer*

KATRINA *Anna's mother*

NINOCHKA *Anna's neighbor*

CONSTANTIN *Carpenter*

ACT ONE

SCENE 1

A field in Siberia. The present.

KATRINA: Listen.

ANNA: What is it?

KATRINA: The song of the Lark.

ANNA: I hear it.

KATRINA: It is beautiful.

ANNA: Is that the sun?

KATRINA: It is the moon.

ANNA: It is red.

KATRINA: I see it.

ANNA: Why did we stop walking?

KATRINA: To listen.

ANNA: And to look at the red moon?

KATRINA: Yes.

ANNA: What does it mean?

KATRINA: It means that you and I are together.

ANNA: It is good.

KATRINA: Yes. We will always have it.

ANNA: Yes.

KATRINA: Yes.

(Fadeout)

SCENE 2

The Actors Café in Siberia. Anna is dancing to Billie Holiday's "Body and Soul." As she dances she is crying. Ivan is watching Anna dance. Natasha is sitting in his lap. They are drunk. They are dressed in blue jeans and tee shirts. Dimitry is sitting alone at a table. He is wearing a suit.

IVAN: *(He sings along with the music.)* That's right! And how! She can say that again. Come on Natasha, this is good. Kiss me and put your hand there. That's one way I like it.

NATASHA: Me too. Put your hand there.

IVAN: Vodka and the feel of a woman. That's all I need.

NATASHA: Vodka and a man.

IVAN: Oh, baby….

NATASHA: Yeah, man…

IVAN: I know.

NATASHA: The music gets in me, Ivan.

IVAN: You're my girlfriend, Natasha. I don't care.

NATASHA: Shut up. I don't care, either. This is what I live

for. This kind of love.

IVAN: Yeah, shut up. I live for this kind of love too.

NATASHA: This making out is great, huh, Ivan?

IVAN: Yeah….Shut up

NATASHA: Yeah….I don't want to be your girlfriend. Anna's

your girlfriend.

IVAN: I have two girlfriends. You and Anna. Anna does not

like it, but she kisses me anyway so I don't care.

NATASHA: I don't want you to be my boyfriend.

IVAN: I'm not your boyfriend. You're my girlfriend.

NATASHA: I told you I don't want friends. I want to be left alone until I want something. This is what I want now.

IVAN: Good.

NATASHA: My parents are servants for the richest people in town. I am the maid. It is all wanting and wanting and now the teenage boy wants me. He sees me go out in short skirts and it does something to him. The father wanted me too. I do not want to be wanted. I will do all the wanting.

IVAN: All right. I don't want anything.

NATASHA: Good. Put your hands there. Let's kiss....

As the two make out, Anna dances and tears stream down her face. When the song is over she runs off stage. Dimitry watches her go off and stands up. Natasha and Ivan have not noticed as they continue to make out. Anna returns with a gun and points it at them as she trembles and closes her eyes tightly. Dimitry leaps over and grabs her and pulls her over to his table. He takes the gun and sits her down. She runs out into the alley and

Dimitry runs after her. He pulls her back in and sits her back down. Ivan and Natasha are oblivious to it all.

DIMITRY: Anna. Have a drink. (*He gives her a glass of brandy and she drinks it*.) Do you feel better?

ANNA: No.

DIMITRY: I am just a businessman. I do not know very much about these things.

ANNA: You're a liar.

DIMITRY: We are all liars.

ANNA: Profound. I hate your guts.

DIMITRY: I employ you.

ANNA: That is why I hate you.

DIMITRY: It is good that you hate me.

ANNA: I love Ivan. I love him. I'm going to shoot myself.

DIMITRY: What good is being dead?

ANNA: It will make Ivan suffer.

DIMITRY: He is not capable of suffering.

ANNA: It is better than misery.

DIMITRY: Misery is better than death.

ANNA: How do you know?

DIMITRY: I am guessing.

ANNA: I am guessing I will be happy dead.

DIMITRY: What will happen to your mother?

ANNA: She will be sad.

DIMITRY: Do you want that?

ANNA: I do not care now.

DIMITRY: You can kill Ivan and Natasha, I don't care, but not in my place.

ANNA: You don't understand. I love him and look at what he does.

DIMITRY: Why do you love him?

ANNA: Because I do and a million reasons. My skin aches for him. Only him. And when my skin aches and he comes to me and we are done, I can feel my skin glowing like and radiate red. Then he does this. It is not the same for him. I have no choice. Suicide is not a choice, Dimitry.

DIMITRY: I have another idea.

ANNA: What?

DIMITRY: Instead of killing yourself, why don't you go to America?

ANNA: I think I'll kill myself.

DIMITRY: America is good. You can dance.

ANNA: I have no money.

DIMITRY: I can help you.

ANNA: I do not want your help. I'll dance now. It is the only thing that means anything.

DIMITRY: Nothing makes you happy.

ANNA: Nothing makes me happy.

DIMITRY: America can make you happy. Everyone is happy in America.

ANNA: Because they do not know the true pleasure of suffering.

DIMITRY: Nevertheless... They want to be happy. It is set up for them to be happy.

ANNA: I do not want to be happy. I want to dance.

DIMITRY: It is set up for you to dance.

ANNA: In America?

DIMITRY: You will be a great dancer there. People will come
to see you dance. They will be delighted.

ANNA: What do I care if they are delighted.

DIMIRTY: You feel that way now, Anna. But when you are
married and your life is in order, it will be different.

ANNA: Who said anything about married?

DIMITRY: Have another drink, Anna.

ANNA: Look at them. Just look at them. They don't love each
other.

DIMITRY: Have another drink.

ANNA: Hey, you!

CONSTANTIN: (*He has been sitting at a nearby table.*) Who,
me?

ANNA: Do you love me?

CONSTANTIN: What?

ANNA: You love me, don't you? Admit it, you love me.

CONSTANTIN: Yes, I watch you dance and I love you.

ANNA: And you want to kiss me, Constantin. I know you want

> to kiss me because every man wants to kiss me. They watch
>
> me dance and they want to kiss me. It is only natural so do
>
> not deny it.

CONSTANTIN: I would be a fool to deny the truth.

ANNA: It is good to be a fool sometimes. Watch me dance,

> then kiss me. *(Music grows louder and Anna goes back to*
>
> *dancing. Natasha and Ivan continue to kiss. Dimitry at one*
>
> *table and Constantin at another drink and watch Anna*
>
> *dance.)*

Fadeout

SCENE 3

The bar of the Iroquois Hotel, Boston, Massachusetts. The

present.

VIOLET: I met him on a train. Well, I knew him before. We

> met on the train by chance. We took a cab to The Ritz

151

Hotel.   The doorman opened the door for us. We sat in a dark corner of the bar and drank Scotch. He said to do this thing we had better do it right. It was a September day. He looked straight into my eyes, and nothing else existed to him in the world but me. We started before we got in the room, we didn't even get our clothes off.   It was like thunderworks...

MAURA: You mean fireworks.

VIOLET: That too. My skin! Every inch of my skin got tight, tighter and tighter. My brain quit working. It was the most important thing to him and me and his skin got tighter and redder...

MAURA: What happened?

VIOLET: What do you think happened?   Haven't you ever done it like that before. I mean right out of the nowhere like that. I'm Violet Chimes, because my mother heard violet chimes when I was born.

MAURA: I'm Maura Olson, because that's my name. Pleased
   to meet you.

VIOLET: Here's the dirty rotten thing about it?

MAURA: About what?

VIOLET: I fell for him. I couldn't stop thinking about him. I
   can't stop thinking about him.   I'm not a nut or anything, I
   mean, I'm not going to do anything crazy--I don't think. Oh,
   Rupert… His name is Rupert Williams.

MAURA: He's part of that thing that's coming in here tonight?
   It's a very big deal.

VIOLET: Turned out that he took the train into Boston twice a
   week, so we met like that. He was supposed to be someplace
   else and I was supposed to be someplace else but there we
   were together. This went on until I was through with school.
   I went to New York. We shook hands. I can still feel the
   feel of his hand and see his face against the blue spring sky.
   I got it bad, Maura.

MAURA: I see.

VIOLET: I tried to forget him. I swear I did. I threw myself into my work. Worked all the time, days, nights, weekends. I couldn't shake the feeling. His face and hands haunted me. I don't want him to see me.

MAURA: Did you go out with anyone else?

VIOLET: Sure and the more I told them to get lost the more they went for me. They left me cold and blank and feeling nothing.

MAURA: He must be something.

VIOLET: I don't know what I'm doing. I'm hypnotized by love. This is my destiny.   He is the love of my life. Rupert…Rupert…

MAURA: Take it easy.

VIOLET: When does this thing start?   What is this thing? When do they get here.

MAURA: He'll see you.

VIOLET : When he gets here, I'll do something. Where am I? I got a room in this hotel. What is this place?

MAURA: This is the Iroquois Hotel. You're in the Gladstone
Room.

VIOLET: The Gladstone Room?

MAURA: Yes. You're in Boston.

VIOLET: That's right. I took a train here this morning from
New York. I left on the three A.M. from Pennsylvania
Station. I'm a short order cook, you know. I work in an all
night diner called Denise's Night and Silence and Earth

MAURA: Some name for a diner.

VIOLET: In the day I walk all over Manhattan. I have a bed in
the maid's room at my aunt's apartment on Park Avenue. I
sleep on the floor; I shower; I change my clothes and work.
I think of him and go where he goes sometimes when I
know he will be there. And I look at him and he does not
see me and it is a perfect relationship

MAURA: How did you know about this?

VIOLET: What is this?

MAURA: The big night.

155

VIOLET: The big night?

MAURA: You must have read about it.

VIOLET: Yes, I read about it.

MAURA: It was in all the papers.

VIOLET: The papers?

MAURA: Here...here's the Boston Tribune. (*Hands her the paper.*)

(*Valerie L. Valentino enters.*)

VAL: Don't anybody move! Bartender. Scotch. I drink scotch.

MAURA: You told us not to move.

VAL: Shut up! Do you know where we are?

VIOLET: I do. I do. I think. Where am I?

VAL: Quiet! That was a rhetorical question.

MAURA: A what?

VAL: Shhh! Listen.... You can sense his presence. He is here with us. I will breathe him into me.... Yes...I can feel him here. You! Get out of that chair!

VIOLET: Me?

VAL: He sat in this chair. This was his chair; the chair he sat in!

MAURA: The chairs are the same. How can you tell?

VAL: I can see him brooding there. That's what he does—brood. I like a man that broods. Don't you?

VIOLET: I've been up all night. I have a small bed, but I sleep on the floor beside it. Sometimes I put me feet up on it and sleep that way.

VAL: I like your face.

VIOLET: Thank you. But I am sad.

MAURA: What makes you sad.

VIOLET: My face.

VAL: This space is filled with the essence of him. I will luxuriate in him and take my fill and then I will know and see and feel the stark, bitter reality that is…

VIOLET: Me.

VAL: Yes, you! I don't want to know anything about you. Bartender. Scotch. You cannot trust a man who does not drink scotch. Don't you think?

VIOLET: I think that I am consumed by love. I think that every move and thought and word I say is about love.

MAURA: Here you are, ma'am.

VAL: My name is Valerie L. Valentino. Professor Valerie L. Valentino. Saint James College, Cape Saint James, Maine.

MAURA: Bartender Maura Olson. Gladstone Room of the Iroquois Hotel.

VAL: Ahh! The Gladstone Room. How fitting! How right! How perfect! Do you believe in fate? Do you believe in immortality? He sat in that chair? The air in this room boils with him!

VIOLET: I have come here for the love I need now, and it is more important to me than wisdom and money. I am in a quicksand of love but I am alone.

MAURA: Smile and look confused.

VAL: That Scottish play. "A poor player that struts and frets his hour on the stage…"

VIOLET: My mind has conceived my love.   The mind conceives the love and the dimensions register in the senses.

VAL: Nobody move!   The juice of his imagination is in me.   I am a red moon tonight! Get me! A red moon! And when a person is a red moon, nothing can go wrong.

(*Walter March enters with Corey Cain.*)

WALTER: So I said, you ought to join the committee, it's great…

COREY: What's so great about it?

WALTER: That's what he said, what's so great about it?

COREY: And what did you say?

WALTER: I said plenty!

COREY: You said plenty?

WALTER: Plenty.

COREY: Like what?

WALTER: Like, you get to meet in the Dean's office where you can get a cup of coffee right from the coffee pot in the outer office. Good, strong, black coffee.

COREY: That's swell.

WALTER: And you get to take a gander at the Atlantic Ocean.

COREY: A gander?

WALTER: Yeah. A gander.

COREY: What else?

WALTER: What do you mean, what else, Corey? The Atlantic Ocean's enough of anything.

COREY: You mean you join a committee for the coffee and the view?

WALTER: And the fact that after you make recommendations and decisions, half of your colleagues don't talk to you for at least two years afterwards--so it works out quite nicely.

COREY: Bartender. Two highballs. You want a highball, right, Walter?

WALTER: *(Nods in agreement.)* I tell you it's getting downright, something over at Cape St. James.

COREY: It's always downright something.

WALTER: I know what you mean.

COREY: What is it this year, Walter?

WALTER: I always like to look at the bright side of things.

COREY: What's the bright side?

WALTER: I'll tell you, Corey. This bartender is the bright side. Hello, Bright Side!

MAURA: Watch it, Professor!

COREY: He's watching it, all right.

WALTER: And he likes it, Bright Side.

MAURA: You can call me Up Side.

WALTER: Up Side?

MAURA: Yeah, you say one more thing to me and I'll smack you *Up Side* the head.

WALTER: You hear that Val? There's some lines for your play. Bartender, give that women a drink.

VAL: Look, you, shut up about me and my plays! Let me tell you something, I'm getting that money, see. I'm winning it because this is my year to get it; and no two-bit, lousy, stinking, rotten little poet, which is you, has a snowballs chance in heck! I'm a god damn red moon tonight, see! So shut up!

COREY: Red moon?

VAL: Yeah, that's right, red moon.

VIOLET: Are you all college professors? Rupert is a professor of the middle-ages.

WALTER: Middle-ages of what?   Come on, Val, you know the score.

COREY: What score?

MAURA: Four score and seven years ago…

MARCELLO: (*Enters. He is a Latin lover type who moves smoothly into the room and sits at the bar. He looks at Violet and speaks to her.*) Elegant enchanting eyes you have. Charming. *(Whispers a password.)* Siberian women?

VIOLET: Do I, or are you just saying that, Professor?

MARCELLO: Not a professor, lover I am. One must make love to a lecture, to a class, to whatever does one. (*Whispers.*) Siberian women.

COREY: You mean Siberian Husky.

WALTER: The days of wine and roses are over.

COREY: You said it! This is the last bastion of freedom and good healthy competition! I like it!

WALTER: The best thing about the days of wine and roses being over is you get to say things like the days of wine and roses are over.

COREY: But this! Let's drink to Mrs. Lincoln, no relation to Honest Abe.

WALTER: To Mrs. Lincoln, no relation to Abraham.

COREY: The last rich broad with a sense of humor.

WALTER: You said it! Sense of humor is right, every year her dirty little grant goes to that ridiculous, pathetic, miserable, troubadour minstrel type idiot. Yeah, the last wealthy dame who ain't afraid to have a drink. And she drinks plenty to think that guy can sing.

COREY: He makes her cry.

MARCELLO: Understand me, you do not. I am misunderstood—so misunderstood…

VAL: Listen you! It's going to be different this year. No one's making a monkey out of me. And I say that because I like saying things like that.

WALTER: Yeah, but why do we have to hear it?

VIOLET: His voice does something to me. When he sings his voice is gentle.

MAURA: Be careful, kid. These people are very nervous. Almost a million dollars is at stake. Each one of them has to prove why their project should get the money. Every year Rupert Williams will come in and melt Eileen Lincoln's face.

VAL: Shut up! This year is different. This year I am a red moon and a red moon means luck.!

COREY: You can say anything you like.

WALTER: You can think anything you like.

MAURA: You can believe anything you like.

VIOLET: But the truth is the truth no matter what. And the truth is I love him. I've always loved him. I always will love him. He took me to Saugus Iron Works. They have this little museum with antique iron things. They have a little slide show on the history of the iron works. We kissed in the dark.   No one else was there. I like to kiss men when historical information is in the air. I took history in college. It was like the world was making love to me and the history professor would look at me and it was my first affair and it was good.

LENNY: (*Enters and canvases the room with his eyes. He wears a fedora hat and a dark suit.*)

MARCELLO: Marcello, am I, and I teach amour history. I have lips professional. I would like to place my lips on your thighs. I am professional. It is very historical.

VIOLET: You do? I mean, you do…

MARCELLO: Yes. My desire is that. *(Whispers.)* Siberian Women.

LENNY: *(He sits next to Marcello but does not look at him. He speaks to Maura.)* You. Beer.

MAURA: Me. Maura.

LENNY: Everybody is a wise guy. *(He whispers from the side of his mouth to Marcello.)* Siberian Women.

VAL: This is my year, and I'll tell you why this is my year. It's quite simple really.

WALTER: You're a red moon.

COREY: A red moon means luck.

VAL: I have written a play—a masterpiece! My masterpiece! It has the soul of Eugene O'Neill; let me tell you it is a tortured soul. I have suffered. I suffer. It is my fate to suffer. Have you ever suffered? Really suffered. No, no, don't say anything. I had to suffer to write my play. I had to know the immediacy of it, of squalor and poverty. To have nothing! Oh, the irony of it! What will come of it? I'll tell you.

COREY: Don't tell us.

WALTER: Poverty?

MAURA: What irony?

VAL: It is the summit of irony! But I must save it. I must hold on to it. I must not let the cat out of the bag; spill the beans. No, I must wait, wait, wait until it is my time, my turn. The time is not right. But tonight, soon, soon, you will be amazed!

MELODY: *(She is a prostitute who storms into the room and slams her pocket book on a table and crosses her arms. Maura automatically brings her a drink. Melody drinks it down and Maura brings her another.)* Look around you. Look around. Here I am. I keep telling the world I am here, but it doesn't seem to matter. The world doesn't care and why should it? I shoulda' gone to college. Yeah, that would have made the difference. Say! That's it! I figured it out!

If the world don't care about me, maybe I oughta' care about the world. Maura, you know any good colleges around here?

MAURA: These here are college profs, Melody, ask one of them.

MELODY: Profs?

MAURA: Professional college professors.

MELODY: No kidding? All of them? It's serendipity, I tell you.

MAURA: Serendipity.

MELODY: This some kind of professor thing?

MAURA: Yeah, it's a professor thing and they chose my place to have it and you know why?

MELODY: I get it, a convention. How do you like that, a genuine college type convention right here at the little old Gladstone Room of the Iroquois Hotel

WALTER: Because Mrs. Lincoln, no relation to the beard, has a vivid sense of humor.

COREY: You'd think she would hire a hall at the Ritz or Copley Plaza?

MAURA: Now just a minute! Do you know who sat in that chair?

COREY: Which chair?

MAURA: That chair.

WALTER: Where?

MAURA: The one over there.

MARCELLO: Oh, yes, vivid are you. You look vivid very to me.

VIOLET: I am vivid.

MARCELLO: You are vivid. There is something vivid about you.

VIOLET: There is something vivid about you, I mean me.

LENNY: (*Whispering to Marcello as he drags him to another table.*) Sit down here and keep your trap shut.

MARCELLO: But only I was …

LENNY: Yes, yes, you was only....I should ought to knock your teeth right down your throat.

MARCELLO: Me forgive. I am sorry. I nothing am but a filthy, crushed cigarette butt in the gutter in the rain.

LENNY: And do not forget it!

MARCELLO: Yes, Si. What is the upset?

LENNY: The what?

MARCELLO: You know, the upset. What is, how you say, going up?

LENNY: You mean the setup.

MARCELLO: Si, Si...and when do we go down?

LENNY: Be quiet. I am assessing the situation.

MARCELLO: Oh, yes, Si. That is good. I will sess it as well too also. I will sess the women.

LENNY: Shut up!   Do not assess until I tell you to assess. There is too much assessing and not enough action. I will be done evaluating when I am done evaluating..

MARCELLO: Very good, and I will evaluate the legs.

VIOLET: My legs?

MARCELLO: Yes…

COREY: All the chairs are alike. How can you tell?

MAURA: The chair right over there.

VAL: This one. It is this one. Eugene Gladstone O'Neill sat in this chair. And when I place my behind in it I can feel his torture. Do you believe in immortality?

MARCELLO: *(Speaking to Val.)* I love believe in which I must to be as I am a professional professor lover. Your skin is radiant. I will kiss your hand, every place on your hand with my lips…

VAL: I haven't time for love right now. I'm too busy suffering and liking it.

WALTER: I ain't seen you at no faculty meetings, Ricky Ricardo.

COREY: I ain't seen you at no…. You call yourself an English professor. Almost a million bucks tonight. Almost one million bucks.

171

MELODY: Did you say almost a million dollars.

WALTER: That's what he said. A million American Pie bucks.

I speak American, pal.

COREY: You speak stupid, buddy.

LENNY *(Dragging Marcello back to the table.)* What is the

matter with you! Stop that crazy love business!

MARCELLO: I cannot myself help. Love is my business. I am

in the business of love. It is the only crazy business to be in.

I am consumed with love. Love consumes me. I want to

kiss the mouth of a women. I need my mouth to be next to a

women's mouth. My lips beside her lips. Oh, it is a thing

beautiful—and I need it.

LENNY: I will put my fist on your lips if you do not shut up.

MELODY: Who does a kid have to murder to attain that almost

a million, mister?

COREY: Doctor, Mister…I mean Mister, Doctor…

WALTER: What he means is to get the almost a million

smackers you have to get it.

COREY: That is, prove you almost deserve it to Mrs. Eileen Somerset Lincoln, whose dear old alma mater happens to be Saint Cape James College which is where we happen to be professors at thereof.

MELODY: This interests me. Let me get it straight. Where was I last year when this little shindig was taking place and otherwise happening in the Gladstone Room of the Iroquois Hotel where I happen to be a resident of said same hotel?

VAL: Don't listen to them. They don't know what they're talking about. They happen to be knuckleheads. I'll tell you how it's been before, but first I'll tell you how it will be tonight.

WALTER: She asked me.

COREY: She was talking to me. And may I say she is charming. I am Professor Corey Cain. You are charming.

MELODY: I'm Melody Place, and I am charming.

VIOLET: What a lovely word, charming. People don't say charming enough anymore. That's my problem. I am charmed too, too easily. It is Rupert Williams. He has charmed me and I am ruined. Charming means positive but unpredictable.

MELODY: Rupert Williams?

VIOLET: Yes, Rupert is the song in my head and heart that I cannot shake.

VAL: Rupert Williams, Rupert Williams, that two-bit, measly little creep. Tonight! Tonight! His reign will be over and he will embrace me for my masterpiece, my great play; the play written with the spirit and soul, the deep, dark soul of Eugene O'Neill who sat in this chair—this chair on which I sit presently and forthwith, with my own deep, dark, tortured…

MELODY: Behind.

VAL: Soul….

MELODY: You wrote a play? No kidding? Gee, that's swell. I love the theater. I always wanted to be an actress. Maybe you could use your influence and put me in one of your plays.

VAL: I need to be left alone.

VIOLET: Oh, Rupert, Rupert…

VAL: Rupert! Rupert! Rupert!

WALTER: When Mrs. Eileen Somerset Lincoln arrives, with her two lovely nubile daughters whom she is currently, presently looking for a husband for, a different husband for each one that is, because they have just recently attained and reached that ripe young age of consentment, the proceedings will proceed. When the very, very rich and large women comes, we the undersigned, that is us college professors from Cape St. James College, that third-rate school on the rocky, rocky coast of Maine, will commence and begin to individually and alone present our case, our project, our study, our endeavor, our art thing to Mrs. Somerset Lincoln, no relation to…

COREY: The one she likes best, gets the almost a million bucks.

WALTER: With which they can spend as they please.

COREY: On the project, that is.

WALTER: On the project that is.

VAL: Siberia. Siberia. It is all about Siberia! Something tells me to speak of Siberia, to speak of Siberian women.... Tundra...

MARCELLO: Hey! That's it!

LENNY: Not here! Not now! Not yet!

MARCELLO: But!

LENNY: Quiet!

VIOLET: Oh, Rupert. I long for, Rupert. But he must not see me. Maura. Where can I hide? He will be here and I will hide. He is a man-angel. His eyes. His lips. His velvet voice...

VAL: I see peasant women in dark wooden houses....The women build fires in the night in Siberia...

(Fadeout)

<u>SCENE 4</u>

The Actors Café. Dimitry and Anna are seated at the table.
There is no one else in the café. It is late and it has closed.

DIMITRY: It is really quite simple.

ANNA: Everything is quite simple.

DIMITRY: Yes, everything is quite simple. You only sign one
thing.

ANNA: I sign one thing

DIMITRY: That is right. That is all you have to do. It is very
simple.

ANNA: Then what?

DIMITRY: You get on the eight o'clock train for Moscow.
Here is your ticket. (*He hands her a ticket and she looks at
it.*) I will drive you.

ANNA: One way.

DIMITRY: One way.

ANNA: One way.

DIMITRY: I man will meet you. He will find you. He will give
you a passport. You will take it. Your name will be Jane.
You will give him this envelope.

ANNA: Jane.

DIMITRY: You will answer to Jane.

ANNA: Jane.

DIMITRY: He will take you to a plane and you will get on it. You will have a small bag with a few of your belongings. You will take them on the plane.

ANNA: A few belongings.

DIMITRY: A few belongings.

ANNA: Yes.

DIMITRY: Yes.

ANNA: I will dance.

DIMITRY: You can do anything you like in America.

ANNA: You can do anything you like in America.

DIMITRY: You can dance and another man will meet you at the airport in New York. You will give him this envelope.

ANNA: I don't care.

DIMITRY: Your mother will not have to work anymore.

ANNA: Yes.

DIMITRY: And you can dance and the man will put you in a taxi which will take you to a place in Manhattan where another man will meet you. You will give him this envelope.

ANNA: This envelope.

DIMITRY: The envelopes are the same. Do not open them. You can dance in America.

ANNA: I can dance in America.

DIMITRY: You will be a dancer.

178

ANNA: I am a dancer.

DIMITRY: What you are doing is good.

ANNA: What will I become?

DIMITRY: You will become what you will become.

ANNA: Good-bye

DIMITRY: Good-bye. Oh, I almost forgot. This envelope is for you.

ANNA: Thank you.

DIMITRY: You may open that one.

ANNA: Thank you. Good-bye, Dimitry.

DIMITRY: Good-bye, Anna.

ANNA: What am I doing?

DIMITRY: It is very simple really. It is nothing.

ANNA: It is nothing?

DIMITRY: Nothing.

ANNA: Dimitry?

DIMITRY: Yes?

ANNA: I want to know one thing.

DIMITRY: One thing?

ANNA: Yes.

DIMITRY: What is it?

ANNA: I want to hear it.

DIMITRY: Hear what?

ANNA: I need to hear the words.

DIMITRY: It is not important.

ANNA: It is important.

DIMITRY: Why? You will still have choices.

ANNA: Will I?

DIMITRY: You will be free in America. Only…

ANNA: Only I signed a paper.

DIMITRY: Yes. You will be loved in America. It will be like love.

ANNA: Anything else?

DIMITRY: Can it be worse than Ivan?

ANNA: No. I suppose not. I love him. I love him. It cannot be worse.

DIMITRY: Until, tonight then.

ANNA: Tonight….

(*Dimitry exits. Anna sits alone as the lights fade.*)

SCENE 5

The main room in a small wooden house in Siberia.

ANNA: (*Writing a letter at the table*) Dear Mother, I am afraid that the situation has become unbearable, no, scratch that out. Impossible. Yes, it has become quite impossible and I can no longer endure. Yes, that is good. It is good to write things like, I can no longer endure. I cannot go on this way any longer. I love Ivan too much to see him with another girl because he will never marry me because he drinks and loves all kinds of girls too much and his life is too hard and too miserable to love me the way I need to be loved. I need to be loved by a man, mother, but not the way it is with him. I see him in the Actors Café when I dance after work. I see him laughing. Something is always funny with a girl sitting in his lap and her hand somewhere in his clothes and his hand somewhere in her clothes and they have cigarettes between their lips. Then later at night he comes to me and I can smell perfume on him and taste her on his mouth and even though there is something about it I like, it is no good. It is not the kind of thing I want anymore. It is the kind of thing only good for a time. Besides I am twenty-one and I am not a girl anymore and I must find out about the world. My blood aches to know the world. My blood demands adventure and I am restless--it is time for me to be on my own. It is time. Papa is dead. The best times are over. Everyone says so. The farm is no good. It never was any good anyway. You are tired and work double shifts. Our only pleasure is the garden in spring when we work on it together, dig in the earth, and sit in the cool dusk and grab handfuls of lettuce and eat it like the Roman gladiators. That, and tea with you, mother. I sigh because I have signed a paper and there is no turning back. I am going through with it. The train leaves for Moscow tonight, before you come home. I will be on that train. I will come back for you, Mama, someday when I have made something of myself in America. One cannot be a dancer in Siberia. All you can be is a peasant. I am through dancing barefoot in the Actors Café. I know that no one ever comes back to Danchenko. No one ever comes back to Siberia. But remember, Mama, that time in the field we heard the song of the morning lark and saw the red moon. That is luck, mama. I am lucky. I know it in my bones. So I must go. It is time.

I signed the paper. Dimitry said it is good. I have made a
promise and there is no turning back. Signed, your loving
daughter, Anna

(She puts the letter in an envelope and places it on the table.
Puts on her hat and coat, picks up he suitcase, and starts for the
door.   Before she can leave her mother enters with their
neighbor.)

KATRINA: So I said to the big idiot, nobody tells me what to
do! And you are the biggest, fattest nobody of all! How
many bosses are there? How many bosses do we have to
have? I mean is everyone our boss? I ask you Ninochka.

NINOCHKA: From our position, everyone is on top.

KATRINA: Yes, but average people switch off now and then.

ANNA: Mother, listen to me.

KATRINA: Anna, you tell Ninochka what I said to the last
supervisor who told me what to do. I know what to do. And
this one was a supervisor in another sector.   You tell

Ninochka, Anna. Tell her I know what is right and wrong!
And when I'm right. I happen to be right!

ANNA: Mother I...

NINOCHKA: Anna doesn't have to tell me, Katrina. I've lived
next door to you for twenty years. They ought to make you
supervisor, Katrina. That's what they would do if they had
any guts and brains. You'd be a good supervisor.

ANNA: Mother...

KATRINA: Me! Never! You have to keep records on people!
You have to be like Stalin, like some crusty old communist.
I don't believe in keeping files with a persons record in it.
Because it is all lies. Even the good things are lies. The
truth is the present. The past is too easy to fabricate! I say
no files. No records! Only people now!

ANNA: *(Hugs Katrina and starts for the door again.)* Good
bye, Mama...

KATRINA: What time you will be home, Anna?

NINOCHKA: Why do you have a suitcase, Anna?

KATRINA: Suitcase! You are not moving in with Ivan!

ANNA: I'm not moving in with Ivan.

KATRINA: You said it! And *how,* you are not moving in with Ivan! And you're not going to marry him either. I'll remind you of that right now! You should marry Dimitry. Dimitry is a gentleman.

ANNA: I know that about Dimitry.

NINOCHKA: Where are you going, Anna?

ANNA: It's in the letter. Good bye! Let me go!

KATRINA: What letter? Tell us!

NINOCHKA: This letter?

KATRINA: You pack your suitcase and write me a letter! Would you pack a suitcase and write a letter if your father was alive?

ANNA: I signed a paper. I promised.

KATRINA: What paper? What promise? You don't discuss this with me? You just write a letter, pack a suitcase, sign a paper like that!

ANNA: There's no time! I have to be on the eight o'clock train.

KATRINA: Train!

NINOCHKA: Why don't you read the letter, Katrina?

KATRINA: Because I don't need to. I know everything! And I know that Anna is not getting on the eight o'clock train!

(Fadeout)

SCENE 4

MELODY: I like it. It's cute. Almost a million bucks for proposin' to do something. This gets me thinking. I got a couple of projects I'm working on. What I could do with almost a million bucks...Why I'd quit this business in a flash. You think anybody consciously chooses to be a prostitute? You think that was my childhood dream? Well, it wasn't.

WALTER: Say, Val. More competition for you.

VAL: I laugh in the face of competition because I have no competition. Why? Because I am a splendid playwright. I love the word, splendid.

EILEEN: (*Eileen Somerset Lincoln enters. She is a middle-aged women of grand stature. Her expression is of one who sees the marvelous joke of life. She is followed by her daughters, Hazel and Adele. Hazel is riding a bicycle and she keeps riding around the room. Adele chain smokes.)* Oh. Yes. I have arrived. Miss. Olson, so good to see you again. But where is Rupert? Where is Rupert Williams?

VIOLET: Where is Rupert?

WALTER: Have you got your check book, Mrs. Lincoln?

EILEEN: (*Laughing at Walter's joke.*) Eileen, boys, call me Eileen. Tonight….Tonight is the night!

COREY: You said it, and how! Mrs. Lin…I mean Eileen. Wait until you hear my proposal, Mrs. L., just wait!

ADELE: Well, well, well, well, well, well, who is this? Don't tell me. I will find out for my little old self. (*She sits next to Marcello.*)

Dan Sklar

HAZEL: Pay no attention to me. This is what I do because I do this. I am free and I am over twenty-one and mother says it is time for me to get married.

ADELE: That's right, Mr. Man type person. Mother wants me to get married too. But with you, let's skip the married part.

MARCELLO: You are a model, no? You must be a model. Do not tell me you are not a model.

ADELE: Name's Adele Lincoln. Give me a cigarette, would you. Never mind, I've got my own. That there is my mother. And that nut you see riding on the bicycle is my sister, Hazel. Here is my hand. Do whatever you want with it.

MARCELLO: Kiss it, I will, with my lips.

ADELE: Be my guest. Oh, that is nice, very nice...

LENNY: What do you think you are doing!?

MARCELLO: What does it look like I am doing?

LENNY: It looks like you are making a spectacle of yourself.

MARCELLO: I am because love is beautiful and...

LENNY: Shut up and put those lips away!

ADELE: Keep those lips where they are!

HAZEL: It is true. I am the only free person in this room. But mother wants me to get married so my freedom will end and I will no longer be myself. I will be dead. But for now, I ride and I am free. I ride my bicycle because I am rich. I ride and sit on the beach in the winter. I ride and go to museums when everyone else is at school. Museums and the beaches and the woods are my teachers. The beaches are my teachers. The beaches are my teachers.

MAURA: Now that Mrs. Lincoln is here and has arrived, it is time forthwith to start and commence. Ladies and Gentlemen, as owner and operator and manager of the Iroquois Hotel, and here in the Gladstone Room wherein Eugene O'Neill often used to drink himself into a stupor, in that chair, of which I am proprietator, lock, stock, and barrel, that is of the Iroquois Hotel and Gladstone Room to which I am chief cook and bottle washer, I would hereby…hereby…begin and…. And though although I ain't much, that is, I am not much for being too good at making speeches, leave us proceed with the proceedings.

VAL: Yes. It is time to begin because this is the beginning and that is the place to start. Where does the horizon begin and where does it end? My Siberian women are in a field and there is a broad horizon as the curtain opens…

MELODY: I was in Nevada once, at a casino. It was sunset. I went outside and saw this sunset behind the desert mountains. No one else in Las Vegas saw it but me. It was red and made the hills and rocks red. I guess people choose slot machines over sunsets.

HAZEL: That's because people choose fake things over real things.

WALTER: Slot machines are as real as any sunset.

COREY: Wait a minute. We can't proceed.

WALTER: We can't proceed.

COREY: Whose got the list?

WALTER: What list? There ain't no list.

COREY: What do you mean there ain't, I mean, there isn't any list? Of course there's a list.

WALTER: I tell you there's no list. Does this look like the kind of place that would have a list?

COREY: There's a list of the proceedings. We all signed it and wrote an abstract of our thing.

WALTER: Thing?

COREY: Project.

WALTER: I never signed any list. I wouldn't be doing this if I had to be on some list.

COREY: You signed the list.

WALTER: I didn't sign nothing.

COREY: You certainly did. Tell him about the list, Val. Whose got the list?

MAURA: I got a list right here.

COREY: You see that.

Dan Sklar

WALTER: See what? Let me see that. *(Grabs the list.)* It's a list of stuff she needs for the bar. Oranges, cherries, a case of vodka, case of...

MAURA: Put limes on that list, would you. Whose got a pencil or pen?

WALTER: This list will do! Now we got a list. You happy?

COREY: No, I'm not happy. That list stinks.

MAURA: Now just a minute. That happens to be a very important list.

EILEEN: Have you gentlemen met my daughters?

VAL: The question is, should I be first or last or somewhere in the middle? I will look to the moon, the red moon, for the answer.

WALTER: It takes a small mind to want his name on a list.

COREY: There has to be some sort of structure, some organization to this process. I mean rules. Say, who are you calling small minded?

EILEEN: The proceedings are informal gentlemen. You tell us why your project is good and if I like it, I write you a check, for almost a million dollars, to do with what you please. It is really quite simple. Shall we continue to keep it simple. But we must not go any further until that lovely and delightful and charming and dashing young fellow, Rupert Williams, makes his entrance.

VAL: Everything is Rupert!

VIOLET: Yes, Rupert. He is the only one. Rupert…. Just the mention of his name makes me faint. I work over the fire that feeds America. I am a short order cook in a New York City diner. I sweat and cook and cry and suffer for Rupert. Oh, my Rupert…I suffer and love it. Love is torture.

MELODY: Is it as simple as that? I mean, really that simple? Boy, because if it is, that's for me. I want to live a simple life, see, that's all I want.

EILEEN: Of course it's not simple, dear. But I like to think it is simple.

HAZEL: It is simple, mother, whether you think so or not. It is as simple as a bicycle rider.

ADELE: It is as simple as this delightful stranger kissing my hand.

MARCELLO: I need not food or drink when I have this hand, your hand, to place my lips thereon upon.

LENNY: I do not believe this is happening.

MELODY: Believe it , mister. This is the Gladstone Room of the Iroquois Hotel where everything happens.

VAL: And there is a red moon tonight; and the sun is rising in Siberia and a Lark is singing her morning song. But there are also crows squawking, and for the Siberian women in the field, it will be a dark, dark day.

LENNY: Siberian women, Marcello.

MARCELLO: Yes, I heard it. Siberian Women.

VAL: Siberian Women and the Red Moon.

(Fadeout)

SCENE 5

Lights fade up on the room in the house in Siberia. Anna,

Katrina and Ninochka are as they were before.

ANNA: You are not going to read my letter?

KATRINA: Have you made supper?

ANNA: I wrote a letter to you, mother.

KATRINA: You could have made supper.

ANNA: I signed a paper and I made a promise.

NINOCHKA: Listen to her, Katrina.

KATRINA: Never mind. I will make it. Are you dancing
   tonight?

ANNA: Good-bye. (*She heads for the door and waits for
   something from her mother.*)

KATRINA: I will wait up for you.

NINOCHKA: Katrina, she is leaving for good. Where are you
   going?

ANNA: To America. I am going to America, Mama.

KATRINA: Will you have supper at the Actors Café?

195

NINOCHKA: What are you going to do in America?

ANNA: Dance.

NINOCHKA: How will you live?

KATRINA: Do you need money for tonight?

NINOCHKA: What did you sign? What promise did you make?

KATRINA: There is some money hidden under some papers in the shoe box in the closet.

ANNA: I will not need it.

KATRINA: Take all of it.

ANNA: I said in the letter that I will come back.

KATRINA: I'll get it for you. *(She gets the money.)*

NINOCHKA: Is it a good promise or a bad promise, Anna?

KATRINA: Take it. *(She puts the money on the table.)*

ANNA: It's all the money you have, Mama.

KATRINA: I was thinking about our garden today. You know it really warms me when I think about it. Do you want to get some firewood from the shed, or should I? I'll go. I think we have enough to last the winter. Give me a kiss, Anna. I will wait up for you. But if I am asleep when you come in, wake me.

ANNA: Good-night, Mama. *(She kisses her mother and they hug and kiss again.)*

KATRINA: Good-night. *(She exits to get the firewood.)*

NINOCHKA: What are you waiting for? Go. You have a train to catch. Whose car is that waiting for you out there? Is that Dimitry's car? Is he taking you to the station? Are you going to America with Dimitry?

ANNA: He is just taking me to the station.

NINOCHKA: What are you waiting for? Is it a bad promise?

ANNA: It is a promise.

(BLACK OUT)

<u>SCENE 6</u>

The Gladstone Room

MELODY: Slot Machines and sunsets, yeah, that's it, Mrs. Lincoln. I got a project thing that'll knock your socks off, see. I get it. Hey, Maura kid, you don't have to be a professor or nothing does you, I mean do you? I have a million projects and ideas. I just gotta choose the right one…I gotta do something, see, that no broad has ever done. Like for instance, get laid at every historic sight in the country.

MAURA: There ain't no rules.

MELODY: There ain't no rules, eh?

RUPERT: *(Enters and is dressed as a medieval troubadour with bright reds and yellows and greens and purples and tights and the rest. He carries a guitar and sings and plays. He is confident and delighted with himself because he knows the effect he has on women. He strums his guitar and begins to sing and recite.)* The night calls to my blood. The night is my brother and sister. I come in from the night. The night is always beside me. I fill the night with a thousand candle flames that shine and flicker on your perfect, smooth, glowing, face. *(As he enters, Violet hides behind Maura and watches him.)*

WALTER: This is murder...

COREY: *(Sarcastically)* Marvelous...

MAURA: Oh, brother...

MELODY: What the heck is that?

VIOLET: He's beautiful...

HAZEL: I am a free spirit! How can you control the stars or moon? Can a man marry a genuine hundred percent all-American red-blooded angel, such as myself? I think not. I do not want me life to be an account number on some computer machine somewhere.

ADELE: Furthermore, moreover, and thus, that is, it is important for all of you to know that I need to be happy, otherwise I get depressed.

MARCELLO: My business is to make you happy.

ADELE: Shut up and make me happy.

RUPERT: (*Singing*) As typical of feudalism as armored knights and stone castles are the troubadours. Yes, the troubadour, the minstrel that are I, me, that is. Songster of the middle ages. I am the poet who is a skilled instrumentalists and composer as well as one who wonders from castle to castle, from village to village, from city to city, from suburb to suburb, from mall to mall, from college to college, telling my tales and spinning my yearns and singing my poems and ballads for you…

WALTER: Pardon me while I go throw up.

COREY: Me first.

VIOLET: Rupert…Oh, Rupert….

MAURA: Easy girl, take it easy.

VAL: This, my fine feathered friends and ladies and gentlemen is…

EILEEN: Ahhh, Rupert Williams, charming, just plain charming.

WALTER: Sickening, just plain sickening.

RUPERT: (*Singing.*) Gather 'round. Gather 'round. Come one, come all, and gather 'round. O, I will tell you a tale. I will sing you a tale, of lovers so true and so blue. I will spin you a yarn of love and of pain, of the joy that is so great we must sigh and cry...

COREY: Next there will be a fair maiden.

WALTER: There's always some damn fair maiden.

RUPERT: A fair, fair maiden with golden hair...

COREY: It's the fair maidens.

WALTER: Not the fair maidens.

RUPERT: Fair maidens, fair maidens. Fair maidens, fair maidens with golden hair. Fair maidens, fair maidens, maidens so fair. Fair...

COREY: If he says fair maiden one more time I'll, I'll...

WALTER: I'll wring his neck!

MELODY: Hold it, mister, let him sing about fair maidens. There ain't nothing wrong with fair maidens. Besides, you don't want to antagonize the old bird do you? She's obviously crazy about the kid. And think of those fair maidens, would ya. Think of the mystery of those long dresses and all those under things and the great quest, yeah, the great quest to get to the Holy Grail.

MAURA: The Holy Grail?

HAZEL: Every guy's looking for the Holy Grail.

VAL: Yes.

ADELE: You may imagine my Holy Grail.

MARCELLO: That is what I am busy doing precisely. It is business my.

EILEEN: Rupert is wonderful. I am delighted to be here again and I welcome you all to this, whatever this is. But I will say this, I am eager to hear of your projects and I will choose the one I feel is the most worthy. And this year, in honor of my daughters, Hazel and Adele, I will be consulting each of them on whose project intrigues and interests them, before I make my choice, selection, and decision.

HAZEL: I choose nothing. I am free until I choose something.

ADELE: I choose this young man. His lips are very talented.

MARCELLO: They are professional.

WALTER: Swell, Professor Lips.

COREY: Mrs. Lincoln. I have a project, plan, that will change the course of America. We talk about community and all that. I have the answer, Mrs. Lincoln, In one fell swoop I can fix everything, I mean everything that's wrong with this country. I have the answer!

MELODY: I've got it! Everybody! Listen to me!

VAL: Yes. It took me a week, a whole week for a character to say yes or no. Every single line. Every word… Siberian wind. Women in the Siberian wind…

VIOLET: Love is longing. I long.

MAURA: I was in love once.

MARCELLO: Siberian women, Lenny….

LENNY: Yes. Siberian women.

ADELE: American women! Which is me. Mother, in a few
minutes I will be ready to listen to the presenters present
their presentations, although I must state out right and
without equivocation that Professor Lips has the upper lip on
this thing. Having said that, I will say this, I have an open
mind.

MAURA: I loved a married man. I probably wouldn't have
loved him if he wasn't married.

WALTER: When do we eat?

COREY: Don't you get?

WALTER: Get what?

COREY: The daughters, the daughters, I tell you! If we work
together, Walter, we can split the money in half—fifty-fifty.
Fifty for you and fifty for me. Get it?

WALTER: Fifty-fifty?

MAURA: He came here to the hotel on his way home from
work. Told his wife he was working late.

HAZEL: I am a fair maiden on a bicycle. Get it, Rupert? Fair maiden on a bicycle. I ride through the woods in search of a knight in rusty armor. I want a knight who I can tell to beat it because I don't trust the motives of any knights. They're in it for themselves. That's how I see it. They get you, and once you're got—they're through with you.

MELODY: Old news, sister, old news.

VIOLET: Old news, but beautiful news.

VAL: Beautiful because it is the great battle between them and us. And sad news because it is my women who lose, my Siberian Women, Mrs. Lincoln. The scene is a beat up, crummy, Siberian café. I call it the Actors Café. I don't know why. Anna is dancing to Billie Holiday because Billie Holiday knows the sadness women feel. Her sadness for humanity. The sadness staring her in the face, right in front of her eyes.

WALTER: I feel like I am Zeus and out of my head is popping Athena, with shield and helmet with owl on it. I'll tell you

what I want. I'll tell you my project. It is this: I want a
sandwich . That's it—a sandwich. I don't care what kind,
just a plain and simple sandwich…

MAURA: We got sandwiches out in the Shakespeare Room,
little sandwiches. I made them myself. There's…

WALTER: No, you don't understand. I'm talking about a
sandwich and nothing else! Maybe a piece of cheese or
cucumber in it. I don't even want to know. There comes a
time in a man's life when that is all he wants—and this is
that time for me.

COREY: Poetry.

WALTER: No poetry. Sandwich!

COREY: This is not the way to do this.

WALTER: Oh, no? What is the way?

COREY: I don't know what you're doing and I don't like it.

WALTER: I'm talking about a plain and simple sandwich.

COREY: I'm talking about what is right and wrong!

WALTER: I am talking about nothing.

MAURA: I am talking about this young man who used to come to the hotel and we would play hotel. He would come at times when there were no guests. The place was ours. He would have a drink at that table and I would be behind the bar and he would strike up a conversation and then he would come over to the bar and lean on his elbows and I would lean on my elbows and our faces would be very close as we talked; and our faces would get closer and closer and closer...

VIOLET: This is a beautiful story.

MELODY: Romance is always beautiful.

COREY: Listen everybody. There has to be order. There has to be a system to this thing. It can't be just willy-nilly.

HAZEL: Willy-nilly, willy-nilly, willy-nilly. Willy plus Nilly equals Freedom W + N = F. I love algebra.

WALTER: Algebra is poetry. Listen to these lines from *Introductory Algebra* written by Barbara Poole: "Our objective in solving the equation is to get the variable alone on one side of the equation."

MELODY: To get the variable alone…

MARCELLO: This is my objective. That is always objective of mine.

ADELE: I am the variable.

HAZEL: I don't want to be anybody's variable.

COREY: Yes, but there needs to be a standard procedure to make sense. You can't say algebra is poetry because you want to believe algebra is poetry.

RUPERT: (*Singing*) Willy-nilly… I like you , oo, oo, oo. Willy-nilly. You're so oo, oo, Willy- nilly, you're so Kooky too. Hey that's a song. I just wrote a song. I'll call it, "Willy-nilly!" Oh, willy-nilly, you're so nutty. Willy-nilly, I'm just nuts for you who who… Come on, everybody, sing with me!

VIOLET: Oh, Rupert…

COREY: That's not a medieval song!

VIOLET: It's wonderful….

EILEEN: (*Talking to Violet who is still hiding.*) I don't believe we've been introduced. In fact, Mr. Cain has a point. There ought to be some semblance of a structure to this thing. Perhaps, I suppose. Everyone should introduce themselves. Yes. That is a fine idea. It doesn't seem too restrictive

MELODY: I suppose...I   suppose .... Suppose I do something...Do something that no one women has ever done before! That's it! But what? What am I good at? I'm good at sex. That's it. Can you go to college for sex and be a professor of sex?

WALTER: Poetry.

COREY: What poetry?!

RUPERT: The poetry of the world! Poetica Mundi. (*Singing.*) As I went out one morning, one morning I went out to the meadow, the meadow, the daisy meadow, covered with daisies, daisies, daises, all white and yellow and yellow and white...

VAL: The fantastic irony is this. From the earth… My Siberian women come from the earth. The Siberian women hear the morning lark in the fields. They know the beauty of the morning—of the world. Under their bare feet there is a blackness deep in the earth; a blackness that changes the world. And in their future there is a blackness. And yet the lark sings and the sun rises and their bare feet hold the ground and feel the flying earth. The earth does not know the sadness of people.

EILEEN: Ah….Siberian women.   Your play, Professor Valentino?

VAL: Yes, my play, that I wrote.

MIRCELLO: Siberian women, Lenny!

LENNY: Yes. But it is not the time to make our move.

ADELE: It is the time to make your move, young man.

COREY: Mrs. Lincoln has the right idea. There has to be an organization to this thing. We take turns talking about our project in a formal platform. And I will begin it.

WALTER: I protest!

COREY: Why?

WALTER: Because I protest! Someone has to protest!

COREY: On what grounds?

WALTER: On this ground.

COREY: Regardless. I am Professor Corey Cain and my project is this. Picture it… Picture this. America tied together into a tight knit community. One great U.S.A The way I see it is, you have to have a vision, to see the big picture in this world—in this life. And for big money you need a big idea. And Mrs. Lincoln, I have that big idea. A big idea to help people, to help the country.

WALTER: The country needs a two dollar sandwich.

COREY: A big simple and beautiful idea; and my idea is this. . .

WALTER: Did someone say something about food?

MAURA: Yes, I did. There is a light dinner in the Shakespeare room.

COREY: Dinner! Dinner! How can you think of eating at a time like this. I have an idea that will change the world.

EILEEN: Oh, it can wait, Dr. Cain. The world isn't going anyplace. Come everybody, follow me to the Shakespeare Room.

COREY: What do you mean the world isn't going anyplace. It's racing through space. I mean all the other planets are dead and this planet is alive. Why? What made the conditions so perfect for life?

MELODY: God.

WALTER: Oh, how insignificant we are in the scheme of the universe and time. I mean the farthest limits of all our senses placed in comparison with infinity are as nothing.

COREY: You had to remind me. Just when I was feeling pretty good, you remind me about infinity and how insignificant everything is. The truth is we mean everything. Therefore there is only the practical, the functional thing to do, and that

is to go and move and accumulate material things because
that is what makes us happy

WALTER: Is that so? I'm telling you that if we achieve a
grandeur for ourselves—it is nothing. How like a speck of
dust is all the accumulation of things of all humans
throughout Time in the sight of infinity.

RUPERT: (*Singing.*) Infinity, infinity, I'm crazy 'bout infinity.
I sing to you, infinity. Bring spring to you, infinity. Infinity,
infinity, we're nothing to infinity…

VAL: What is infinity when kids are starving? What is infinity
when their homes are blown apart by terrorists? What is
infinity when one human being is controlled by another?
What is infinity when a human being is heartbroken?

VIOLET: Infinity is love.

COREY: Infinity is nothing! I'm not talking about infinity!

HAZEL: Infinity is me on a bicycle. It is me as an old lady
riding my bicycle. It is me loading three peanut butter and
jelly sandwiches into a small knapsack and riding to a hill

that overlooks the Atlantic Ocean. It is me alone, sitting under a tree on that hill and reading Damon Runyon stories because nobody else does and someone has to and eating the sandwiches with black coffee I pour from a thermos into a red cup.

ADELE: More poetry! I am going to marry some womanizer like this because idiots like him know how to make me happy. He takes the time to make love. Where is the love making project ? I think someone ought to get that almost a million bucks for knowing how to make love to a women. What is more important than that?

VAL: If this were a play. How would I get out of this scene?

COREY: You would satisfy the audience by letting at least one character present their proposal!

VAL: Go ahead.

WALTER: I've already proposed my proposal—a sandwich, to which I am going to exit to the Shakespeare Room forthwith.

COREY: Don't you want to hear my idea?

WALTER: I told you, I want a sandwich. Hazel, would you care to have a sandwich with me?

HAZEL: A sandwich?

WALTER: Yes, a plain and simple sandwich.

HAZEL: May I ride my bike?

WALTER: Let's ride together.

HAZEL: Yes.

(*He climbs onto her bicycle with her and they ride out.*)

COREY: Hey, I don't think I like that. That gives him an unfair advantage. Come back. Did you see that, Mrs. Lincoln? That's not fair. I hate that guy.

EILEEN: I have another daughter, Dr. Cain.

COREY: But she's with him.

EILEEN: Steal her away, Dr. Cain.

COREY: Look, Mrs. Lincoln, would you just listen to my idea.

EILEEN: Come, come, Dr. Cain. Dinner is served in the Shakespeare Room. This desperation on your part is not at all becoming. Shall we go, exit, and otherwise leave the scene?

COREY: Desperation?

ADELE: Coming, Mother. Don't move those lips mister, I'll be back after I eat. I happen to love eating and I have decided to do it daily for the rest of my life. And as for you Dr. Cain, I would consider any advances on your part to be purely the result of your attraction to me and having nothing to do with this grant awards dinner type affair. Perhaps as the evening wears on and you get tight we can try necking to see how you stack up? Frankly I am becoming bored with lover lips over here. Is it a deal? (*She extends her hand to him.*)

COREY: Is what a deal?

ADELE: Never mind. Shall we, mother?

EILEEN: We shall, daughter? Rupert, my dear. Come sing to us while we dine.

RUPERT: (*Singing.*) Eat, drink, and be merry. Oh, I say, eat, drink and be gay! Eat, drink, and be happy, we're only here for a stay. Oh, eat drink, and be silly. Eat drink and be free. Eat, drink in the sunshine. Eat drink in the shade... (*Eileen, Adele, and Rupert exit.*)

MELODY: Rich people...

MAURA: They ain't like you and me. Let's face it.

MELODY: When you're rich everything in your world is clean. Ever notice that. And when something is worn out, it's replaced. Rich people do what they want when they want. You can talk to me, pal, I'll listen. I'm nobody, I guess. I know I'm a prostitute. I have no delusions. I could give all the rotten reasons I'm like this. But you can read about it in your psychology textbooks. I'll listen, pal. Go ahead, what do you want?

COREY: All right, this is it. My proposal is this. It's a massive works project you see where every main street and boulevard in every town and suburb in the United States will have a trolley car system. That's right, street cars crisscrossing every road in America! Think of it! Everyone works. Everyone has the chance to go anywhere anytime. They run twenty-four hours a day you see. We will be freed from the shackles of the automobile. Monorails too! Do you get it? What do you think?

MELODY: Hmmm? I'm listening.

COREY: Why can't some old woman or man somewhere roll out of bed you see and hop on a street car and head downtown to the store or library or coffee shop or to see the grandchildren without depending on a car? I tell you, it's revolutionary. With that almost a million bucks I can calculate the details, write the plan, lobby the government, inspire the people to rise up and demand the freedom and right to…to…

MELODY: To comprehend the destructive force that is love.

COREY: Right. To…what?

MELODY: Would you have a drink with me?

COREY: Well, I… I'm here for this thing.

MELODY: Yes, but I am sad when I am not talking to another person. I want to listen to you and I want you to listen to me. I'm pathetic. Even in kindergarten I had these crushes on boys. I can't get over any of them. Buy me a drink, would you.

MAURA: Open bar tonight, Melody.

COREY: But I aaa…

MELODY: Don't you know what I'm trying to say?

COREY: I think maybe I'm going to…

MELODY: Not one crush ever worked out for me. I tell you if one crush ever worked out I would be loyal. That's it, loyal. And true to one person. One love. One person. What do you say?

COREY: I aaa…

MELODY: Come up to my room. I know you want to come up to my room. I never went to college. Tell me about college.

COREY: College?

MELODY: Come on. Come with me… (*She takes his hand and pulls him with.)*

COREY: But I…

MELODY: You want to come with me don't you? I know you do.

COREY: I…

MELODY: What's the matter? Cat got your tongue?

COREY: What about the *thing*?

MELODY: The thing ain't going nowhere. Love is better than any *thing*. Talk to me about the street cars. Talk to me about your first kisses and your best kisses. (*They exit*)

MARCELLO: *(Calls after)* I will go with you. I am the one whose lips know what to do.

LENNY: Quiet you idiot. We make our move after they have gone.

MARCELLO: Yes, Si, Si. I am a fool for love. I am a prisoner of love.

VIOLET: Me too.

MAURA: Mrs. Eileen Lincoln has invited you all, participant in this thing or not, to a light supper in The Shakespeare Room. Come at your leisure or whenever you like. I, however, must remove myself and go to serve the guests and people too. You coming Violet?

VIOLET: No. I prefer to suffer and long here.

MAURA: I can't leave you like this. Come on into the kitchen. I'll get you something.

VIOLET: Yes. I am happy in the kitchen. The kitchen is where I belong. It is shiny and clean and dirty and is the smells of food and ovens and warmth. It is warm and it is good. I will go to the kitchen and I will look at Rupert from there and long for Rupert from there.

MAURA: All right. That's fine. Come along. Coming, Val?

VAL: Soon.

(*Violet and Maura exit.*)

MARCELLO: Wait. Come back. Need you I do. Your legs are long and…She is gone. Now I am left only to imagine her and that is good too.

LENNY: Marcello. There she is. Now is our chance. We must act before they come back.

MARCELLO: Yes, but do not hurt her.

LENNY: Shut up.

MARCELLO: No.

LENNY: *(He takes out a script from his briefcase.)* Come on, you.

MARCELLO: No. Cannot do this to a women.

LENNY: Siberian Women.! You. Siberian women.

VAL: I heard you the first time.

LENNY: This is from Siberian Women Incorporated! (*Tears up the script and throws it at Val as he takes out his gun and shoots.*)

Blackout

<u>ACT 2 SCENE 1</u>

The Gladstone Room moments after Lenny has shot at Val.
Marcello and Lenny are wrestling for the gun and Val is trying
to hit Lenny over the head with a bottle.

VAL: Hold him still…. Get the gun.

MARCELLO: Hit him! Do something!

VAL: Stop moving!

MARCELLO: What!? How? Do it!

VAL: Oh, I can't. Oh, man. I am opposed to violence!

MARCELLO: But he is not! Do something.

(Val closes her eyes and slams the bottle on his head. Of course
it hits Marcello.)

(They continue to struggle until Marcello manages to get the gun
and he and Val throw Lenny out.)

VAL: Why did you do it?

MARCELLO: I am too filled with life. I am consumed with
    life.

VAL: You saved my life. What is this about?

MARCELLO: Siberian women. Leave here, you must!

VAL: I can't.

MARCELLO: You have to. There is no choice. And now they
    will kill me. I am no good for this kind of work. I am a
    lover, not a killer. This I told to my cousin Giovanni. He

221

said it is like loving. Killing is like loving. It is the same thing. No! It is not!

VAL: Why me?

MARCELLO: There is no time for talk. Come with me. We will hide—together.

VAL: But my play. I wrote a play! I don't believe this! I finally wrote a play that actually means something and I get shot at!

MARCELLO: There is no choice between life and art.

VAL: Than I choose art!

MARCELLO: Do not be a fool!

VAL: But I am a fool.

MARCELLO: And I am a fool in love. Pathetic I am. I am not a man. A man kills. I cannot face Giovanni. I cannot face my family. I am in disgrace. I must go.

VAL: I can't think....

MARCELLO: Together, we will hide out in hotel rooms. Yes. We will have to moving keep on the run like dogs hunted. That is it. We will stay in hotel rooms together and make love to each other all day knowing that death is near. It will make the love better. *(He holds her hands and talks close to her face seducing her.)*

VAL: It will?

MARCELLO: Yes.

VAL: Yes....

MARCELLO: It is good you say yes. It is good now.

VAL: Yes.

MARCELLO: Let us go. Now!

VAL: Now...?

MARCELLO: You must choose life and love. Our lives have become suddenly tangled.

VAL: Tangled?

MARCELLO: Yes. You are a woman and I am a man and we are tangled.

VAL: Our bones will be tangled.

MARCELLO: You see. Yes. Hotel rooms.

VAL: Hotel rooms. Marcello! It is fate. I am a splendid playwright. I love the word splendid. Eugene O'Neill died in a hotel room. Life in the theater is a life in hotel rooms. I must face that now. I must face reality.

MARCELLO: I am reality.

VAL: No. You are in my dream.

MARCELLO: Yes. I am happy to be in your dream.

VAL: How will we live? No. Never mind that question. I must pick up my portable Underwood typewriter.

MARCELLO: There is no time to lose. Out the back, hurry we must....

VAL: Yes. Back alleys, hotel rooms, me typing in hotel rooms.
Yes… Kiss me. I must be certain. *(Marcello kisses her.)* I
am certain. It is better to kiss a stranger than to die!

MARCELLO: Quickly. We must split and flee and leave too!

VAL: But…

MARCELLO: But what?

VAL: My play! My Siberian women! The red moon! Almost a
million bucks! It is my almost a million bucks! I tell you
it's mine!

MARCELLO: Nothing is yours. Those things are nothing.

VAL: No! I don't believe you. You made all of this up to get
me in bed! It's too fantastic to be real!

MARCELLO: It is a good idea but I am not that clever. Your
play is too sad. You have created great sadness.

VAL: But there is sadness in the world.

MARCELLO: Yes. So why write more sadness? Why make
more sadness?

VAL: Because it is the truth.

MARCELLO: But this is a dream. This is a play and you and I
is characters in it. It is romance. Everything is romance.
There is no almost a million bucks. There is only you and
me in hotel rooms looking out windows at the night. It is
our fate. No choice have we The world is filled with
Lennys and they are after us.

VAL: The world is filled with Lennys.

MARCELLO: And we are together in this.

VAL: Kiss me and I will think of an exit for us!

MARCELLO: Someone is coming. I will kiss you and drag you away!

VAL: That is good! Drag me away. It is good to be dragged away sometimes and now is a good time for me to be dragged and for you to….

MARCELLO: Shut up. (*He kisses her and drags her out before she has a chance to finish talking.*)

ACT 2 SCENE 2

A few moments later in the Gladstone Room. Maura and Violet come running on having heard the shot and commotion.

MAURA: I heard it. Did you hear it?

VIOLET: I heard it too. Like a shot.

MAURA: A gunshot.

VIOLET: Yes. It was like a gunshot.

MAURA: Loud-like blam, you know.

VIOLET: I heard it too, but I don't see anything.

MAURA: Yeah. I don't like gunshot sounds in my place.

VIOLET: I don't like gunshots anyplace. Imagine a world without guns.

225

MAURA: My place is a world without guns and I aim to keep it that way.

VIOLET: Guns are nothing but trouble no matter how you look at it.

MAURA: No matter how you look at it. Another drink, Violet?

VIOLET: Thank you, Maura.

MAURA: You're welcome, kid. You know, I was thinking.

VIOLET: You were?

MAURA: Yeah, I was thinking I kinda like you, see.

VIOLET: I like you too.

MAURA: That's good because you know I own this Iroquois Hotel which makes me sort of a businesswoman, you see.

VIOLET: That's what you are all right.

MAURA: Yeah, I'm a businesswomen and as such I run a business of which I am boss.

VIOLET: It's your business and you're the boss.

MAURA: So I was thinking, being the boss and all and this being a business and not just a place for me to have affairs in with married men, that I gotta make money and make it grow see because in the magazines I read, business magazines that is, they say a business has to grow because that's the nature of the thing, a business that is. Don't ask me why. I'm perfectly happy owning a place that's falling apart and barely gets any customers. But the articles say I gotta grow so I was thinking maybe if you was the cook I could get people to eat in the Shakespeare Room like it was an official type restaurant. And you could live here and sleep in any room you wanted to sleep in. What do you say?

VIOLET: I say yes because I like to say yes to things and I see no reason to say no. When I say no to things I forget all the numbers I am supposed to know and I say yes because I am here and I like it and I say yes because my hands were made to butter toast and crack open eggs and peel open bricks of cheese and cut and chop and cut and chop and scoop mashed potatoes onto plates and pour gravy on meat loaf and boil carrots and string beans and rice and bake pumpkin pies— my hands are meant to do these things so therefore I say yes.

MAURA: Let's shake on it.

VIOLET: Okay. When I shake hands I mean it.

MAURA: Me too. *(They shake hands to seal the deal.)*

ACT 2 SCENE 3

(Eileen and Rupert, arm and arm, enter. Eileen is laughing, as they enter, from some witty thing Rupert has said.)

EILEEN: Oh, Rupert. You're so witty.

RUPERT: I am witty, Mrs. Lincoln. In fact, that makes me think of a song. I'll call it Witty Me. Yes, that's it.

(*Singing.*) I'm so witty, so, so witty. I'm witty and silly and free! I am witty. I am crazy and witty as can be....Witty, I'm so witty. I'm so witty, witty me.

EILEEN: You are a genius, Rupert.

RUPERT: I am a genius and I'm tall too. (*Suddenly noticing Violet.*) Say, I know you.

VIOLET: Hello, Rupert.

RUPERT: You are that fine wee fair lassie, Violet

VIOLET: I am that fine wee fair lassie. And you are that fine big tall lad.

RUPERT: I am that fine big tall lad.

VIOLET: Hello, Rupert.

RUPERT: Hello, Violet.

VIOLET: Hello, Rupert.

RUPERT: That is a great song title: Hello, Violet. I am going to write that song, Hello, Violet. (*Singing*) Hello, Violet. Hello, Violet. Hello, Violet, wee, wee fair lassie...

VIOLET: I like being a fair lassie. You remember me?

RUPERT: Of course I remember you. How could I forget those eyes, that mouth, that face.

VIOLET: And I remember you.

RUPERT: The Saugus Iron Works.

VIOLET: All those rusted iron things. There is nothing more romantic than old things.

228

RUPERT: I sing about old things. Old rusted things left out in the rain, left outside all winter.

VIOLET: The train. When I was younger and got on a train I always expected to meet my true love. Our eyes would meet. There would be chemistry. A gravitational pull. And it did happen. It finally happened and it was you.

RUPERT: The taxi cab.

VIOLET: Yes.

RUPERT: The Ritz Hotel.

VIOLET: Yes.

RUPERT: This makes me want to sing. Whenever something beautiful happens, I want to sing. This is a song I wrote just for you. *(As he begins to sing Hazel and Walter ride on, Adele enters, and Melody and Corey enter.) (Rupert sings an entire song.)*

> There's a song in my heart
> I keep on singing a song there.
> There's a song in my heart
> I sing to you.
> There's a bird in my hand
> and a song in my heart.
> I am singing a song
> with a bird in my hand
> and a song in my heart.

I am singing a song
with a bird in my hand
It's a song and a bird and
a song that is deep
in my heart.
It's a bird and a song
and a song and a bird
in my hand.
I sing a bird song
with a bird in my hand
and song in my heart
with a bird.
I am singing a song
from my heart
with a bird in my hand
And you are that bird
in my hand and that song
in my heart
with that bird in my hand.

(Everyone applauds and cheers.)

VIOLET: Oh, Rupert…

RUPERT: Oh, me…

EILEEN: I am confident when I say that I speak for everyone,
Rupert, when I say, Wow! Thank you, thank you. And now

that everyone has eaten and been entertained, we shall begin. In a nutshell or oyster shell or any sort of shell you like, in one concise and brief and thorough sentence, on a piece of scrap paper or a napkin will do quite nicely, please write your passionate projects and then give the piece of paper to my lovely daughter, Adele, so that she may forthwith place it in this hat.

MAURA: Where's Professor, Dr. Valerie L. Valentino?

EILEEN: Oh, we must have Dr. Valentino's most passionate proposal. Where is Professor Valentino? I understand she has written a splendid play.

WALTER: Because she is a splendid playwright.

COREY: And she likes the word splendid.

MAURA: As proprietor of this here establishment, which is like being captain of a ship, I will take the liberty, if you will, whatever that means, to nevertheless and nonetheless write on a scrap of paper, Valentino's proposal of which I happen to know of, that is.

EILEEN: Very good. You may all begin writing now. (*They get out paper and pencils and write their proposals. Eileen gives them a moment before speaking.*) Pencils down! Adele. The hat. (*Adele goes around the room and each person puts paper into the hat.*) Thank you, dear.

ADELE: You are quite welcome mother. And may I say, before the proposals are read, that I have a proposal of my own for the single professors here, and it is this. But first I must say this. I love to eat and I love to cook and I will cook all day. I don't get fat and I love sex. I mean it's scary. I want a husband. There's no sense in beating around the bush. Unlike my nutty sister here, I want a man to boss me around. I am a college professor's dream. He can go to his little college and do whatever it is he thinks is so important all day, and then come home to me. I'm rich so he can do his little research studies or write his little poems, I don't care what. I'll be busy having babies and cooking food and being barefoot and loving life. Let me see a show of hands. Who is willing here?

WALTER: *(Raising his hand eagerly.)* I am! I am!

ADELE: The young man with the long hair! I like it! What about you Dr. Cain? Shall I consider you as well and also too?

COREY: Hear that Melody, dear.

MELODY: I hear it Corey, honey.

HAZEL: Honey? Dear? What the hell is this?

MELODY: This is love and my project is love.

COREY: Love...

WALTER: How do you like that? Sex has turned him into a human being.

COREY: What's that supposed to mean?

ADELE: Who else? How about you, Mr. Minstrel type troubadour type person?

VIOLET: Oh, Rupert...

RUPERT: Oh, Violet...

WALTER: Me! Me! Choose me!

ADELE: Any other takers? Going once. Going twice. Gone to the kooky guy with the long hair!

WALTER: Hooray! Hooray! I'm rich! I'm free! Can you make sandwiches?

ADELE: Can I make sandwiches?! Come here, I'll show you!
(She grabs him and kisses him then throws him down.)

WALTER: Now that is a sandwich. That's the kind of sandwich I've been talking about!

ADELE: Shall we exit and heretofore vacate the premises, Mr. Man type person.

WALTER: It's Dr. Man type person, and yes we shall because this is the Iroquois Hotel and when a man and a woman are in a hotel such as you and me is are, why then it is only natural to take advantage of the situation and...

COREY: Poetry! Some poet!

WALTER: I am not a poet! I am a human being!   You can call me what you will, but I am not a poet. I am not a statistic or a fact which everyone knows that statistic and facts are more important than the moon and stars because that is how policy is made, not by the beauty of the moon and stars or sunrises or deep woods and grass and rocks. And everyone knows that policy is more important than truth and insight and love and compassion and justice and equality.   This is the students' creed.   Listen to it. "I do not give a damn about grades because they are letters and numbers and not me and measure some odd random thing which has nothing to do with my spirit and soul and world. Your due dates mean nothing to me in this due date world. You will get it when you get it when I am done and not before. Keep your shirt on, I'll do it. Your weird little threats are devised by small minds in small worlds with closed doors and no windows. I only want to learn and I will learn in spite of you and your policies. I will learn what I want to learn when I am ready and when I learn. I only want to learn." I will learn regardless of the fact of *Uncle Tom's Cabin*, which happens to be the play we are mounting at Cape St. James College, this semester and here are some of the great, great lines you will hear in our play: *(He says and acts out the lines with passion.)* "Eva, I come..."   says St. Clare as he is dying.

234

And Legree says to poor old Uncle Tom, "Ain't you mine, body and soul!" And he tells his henchman to flog poor old Uncle Tom to "within an inch of his life!" And when Legree is shot he cries, "I am hit! The game's up!" And of course there is Tom's final speech. And this is it. "Bless de Lord! It's all I wanted. They haven't forgot me! Now I shall die content! Don't call me poor fellow! I have been poor fellow, but that's all past and gone now. I'm right in the door, going into glory! Heaven has come!" And there he goes with little Eva on a white cloud. Yes. It's beautiful. They are dead. And finally, I leave you with the words of Ralph Ellison. "Who knows but that, on the lower frequencies, I speak for you?" Why? Because someone has to! Who are you, Adele?

ADELE: I am heaven on a lower frequency. A am your almost a million bucks!

WALTER: Okay, beautiful!

ADELE: Okay, beautiful!

WALTER: Thanks, Mrs. Lincoln. Your daughter is swell!

ADELE: I am swell! *(They exit grandly.)*

EILEEN: He deserves almost a million bucks! I am delighted!

VIOLET: I love this place.

MAURA: Me too.

HAZEL: That was a close one. The guy was after me. Every guy goes after me. They want to take my freedom away. I'm not interested. I ride my bicycle and that is all, that's that, over and out!

EILEEN: Thank you dear. Swing over here and pull a scrap of paper from the hat, read the name and we shall hear the project. My goodness, the field of players certainly has narrowed.

HAZEL: Gladly, mother. I'll gladly swing around anywhere. *(She rides over, reaches into the hat, pulls out a piece of paper and reads the name.)* And the name is…let me make this out…Melody Place. Is there a Melody Place in the place?

MELODY: I am Melody Place!

EILEEN: Hazel will read your statement and you may elucidate, Miss. Place.

HAZEL: *(Reading.)* "My plan is to get laid in Emily Dickinson's bedroom and thus receive a free college education." That's what it says folks.

EILEEN: How fascinating!

MELODY: That's right! And furthermore me and Dr. Cain and I here have worked it all out. Isn't that right, Professor.

COREY: That's right, Professor. I mean, Melody.

MELODY: I shall be the visiting prostitute at Cape St. James College. The resource on whom the students can write their papers. I am a natural resource. I am better than any book. My life is a book. They can study me, interview me, do whatever they want with me. It'll be educational. I mean I can have an office with a chair and desk. And I will write the story of my life and in one chapter I meet a boy and that boy is crazy about Emily Dickinson. So we drive all the way from Texas, which is where I am originally from, to Amherst on a pilgrimage like to go to Emily Dickinson's house and see her room and all and all the way he's reciting Emily Dickinson poems to me and singing them to the tune of "The Yellow Rose of Texas." Anyhow it was great stopping at motels along the way, drinking, having sex, and smoking cigarettes. That was the life! We got to the house and it was closed and you couldn't go in unless you were some big fat literary muckety-muck. The boy was so disappointed. We were determined to see Emily's room so we hung around Amherst all day. We found a skid row dive bar and drank and smoked and made a plan to break in and fuck in her bed with a cool breeze jostling the white curtains. We were lousy at breaking and entering and we weren't sure what room it was. We were laughing and falling all over each other and dropping the hammer and screwdriver we bought from a hardware store. We got arrested. With a letter from Cape St. James College I reckon I can do research in that room there and fulfill a dream that boy had. I don't care one way or the other, I mean, six of one half a dozen of the other. But since he can't fulfill that dream, someone has to. Corey, I mean Professor Cain, here can show me the ropes of getting it done. And in return for my hard work and sacrifice, the college gives me a free four year education and since I'm writing a book about me, I reckon, I'll get a degree in human nature which is creative writing. There ain't nothing more human than creative writing, because creative writing is about human behavior. Now, if those human's would just behave themselves, we'll be all right. What do you say, Mrs. Lincoln?

EILEEN: I say, charming, simply charming!

MELODY: And my book will be called *Wild Nights,* after Emily Dickinson's poem.

(She recites the poem.)

Wild Nights—Wild Nights!

Were I with thee

Wild nights should be

Our luxury!

Futile—the Winds—

To a heart in port—

Done with the compass—

Done with the Chart!

Rowing in Eden—

Ah, the Sea!

Might I but moor—Tonight—

In Thee!

(*All applaud her performance.*)

    Thank you, thank you. Thank you all very much. I so, so look forward to college. With Professor Cain as my guide and mentor, I intend to row in Eden and moor with thee.

COREY: Yeah.... Boy, I'm glad I'm not married!

EILEEN: Very romantical! I realize romantical is not a word, but I like it.

HAZEL: (*She reaches into the hat and pulls out another piece of paper.*) I don't! But I will continue anyway. Hmm…let's see who's next. Ah! Dr. Valerie L. Valentino. And the paper says, and I quote, "To blow the lid off of the Siberian Women prostitution ring with my new play *Siberian Women and the Red Moon.*"

MAURA: That's about the size of it.

EILEEN: Siberian Women and the Red Moon.... I like the sound of that. Have you a script Miss. Olson?

Dan Sklar

MAURA: What am I Valentino's agent? No.

EILEEN: Pity.

HAZEL: Ah, the fickle finger of fate, huh? You just never know what's going to happen.

EILEEN: Next please.

HAZEL: Okeedoekee. (*She reaches into the* hat *and pulls out another piece of paper.*) And the names is Dr. Corey Cain and it says and I quote: "To plan and promote a streetcar and monorail system crisscrossing every hamlet and village and town and city street and road and lane in the United States of America."

EILEEN: My word! That is quite an undertaking. Most interesting. Well? Dr. Cain?

COREY: Yes? (*He has not been listening. He cannot take his eyes off of Melody.*)

EILEEN: Well?

COREY: Well what?

EILEEN: Have you anything to say?

COREY: About what?

HAZEL: What about bicycles? I'm riding mother! I'm through here. Nobody is talking about bicycles. I have news for you professor, it's not street cars that will save the world, it's bicycles and bicycle riders. I'm off, Mother. I am free and

240

off. Good-bye all. *(She throws the hat into the air and starts to ride out.)*

EILEEN: Hazel, wait, you must help me choose! What do you choose? *(Hazel is riding around.)*

HAZEL: I choose the prostitute, mother. She's the freest person in the house. I like it! Shake up the damn institution, that's my motto. When you're rich, what the heck, might as well shake up some institution. Slap some reality in the face of the college. Give her an office with a desk and chair and paper and pencil too. Maybe even give her a computer!

EILEEN: Shake up the institution and change the world! I like it too, Hazel. It is good that you have wisdom. You go to college to get wisdom; and a kindhearted healthy prostitute is loaded with wisdom. I like it! But alas, what will become of Rupert?

RUPERT: Oh, don't worry about me, Mrs. Lincoln. My new song, "There's a Song in my Heart and a Bird in my Hand" will be a hit! Besides, Mrs. Lincoln, I'm still living and singing quite nicely from the last almost a million dollars. Come, Violet, my wee fair lassie. The Ritz Hotel beckons. Our clean room awaits. It calls to my blood like the night. *(As he exits he sings.)* There's a bird in my hand and a song in my heart and a bird in my hand and a song in my heart with a bird in my hand...*(He and Violet start to exit.)*

MAURA: Report to work tomorrow morning, kid!

VIOLET: Aye, aye, captain.   "There's one God over this earth and one captain of the Iroquois Hotel!"   *(She salutes and exits to catch up with Rupert.)*

MAURA: And don't forget it!

EILEEN: Adieu, Rupert. Hazel, shall we be off?

HAZEL: Climb aboard, Mother!

EILEEN: Here is a check, Melody Place. Good luck!

MELODY: Thank you, Mrs. Lincoln.

EILEEN: You are welcome. Good-bye all. Oh, and here is a check for you Miss Olson. Your hotel is charming.

MAURA: Thank you, Mrs. Lincoln. Anytime you want to hire a hall—here I am are is. Don't forget the Iroquois Hotel and the Gladstone Room and the Shakespeare Room of the Iroquois Hotel where everything can happen. Hey, I like that!   That's our new motto type slogan thing—"The Iroquois Hotel Where Everything Happens!" I like it! It has a ring to it. It's catchy. Don't you think? What do you say, Melody?

MELODY: I say the happy days will pass quickly. I say once the Indians fought here and down came the rain. Our teacher is writing and all the children are singing and I will go now. The whole sky is blue and my pencil is sharp and I am very happy. It is time for us to scram and split and leave as well and otherwise vacate the premises.

COREY: Yes. Hey, wait a minute! What's going on here? I feel like something has just slipped through my fingers; like I had something in my hands. I lost. You won.

MELODY: I won.

COREY: But my idea? Street cars? The future? My vision? Oh, what have I done?

MELODY: You have done a great thing. You have had sex with me. I have what I want. We will share the money. Throw bicycle trails crisscrossing America in your plan and it will be pure and sweet; and come with me now to Emily Dickinson's house now tonight and immediately if not sooner and then we will fly to Texas! Oh, Corey!

COREY: Bicycle trails? Texas?

MELODY: We have to tell my mother the good news, don't we?

COREY: Why Texas?

MELODY: My mother lives in Texas!

COREY: I aaa, I , I , I... Oh, well. Oh, me. Oh, my. Why not? Yes, dear.

MELODY: Yes dear is right! Good-bye, Maura. Send my things up to Cape St. James College in care of Professor Corey Cain! Hello Emily Dickinson! I aimed and I hit the mark! In college I shall read and read and read and read. It will be my chief delight! Good-bye Iroquois Hotel! Good-bye Gladstone Room! Good-bye, Maura! Hello college life! *(She and Corey exit singing "The Yellow Rose of Texas.")*

MAURA: So long, Melody, kid. Now I am alone. Gee, that line sounds familiar. Oh, well. Might as well have another drink before I clean up. Maybe I'll start in the Shakespeare Room. *(She exits.)*

ACT 2 SCENE 4

Anna runs into the Gladstone Room as though she were being chased. She has a suitcase with her. She is out of breath. She pours a drink. She searches the place for a telephone and when she finds one she dials and speaks.

ANNA: Hello…hello…hello! Operator! Operator! Get me Siberia! I want Siberia! I need it. I need it. Yes. Operator. Oh, why oh why is there no operator? Siberia, I tell you.! Russia! What have I done? I am a fool. I should have shot myself. What was I thinking? I must have been mad to have signed that paper. I must have been mad to have taken that money. Now I am really in a fix! Hello. Hello. Get me Siberia! Siberia. I want to go home. I want to go home. I can't go home. Oh, I have made a shambles of my life.

That's it, a shambles. My life is in shambles. Operator! Operator! Please... Please....Mama, mama, I remember the red moon; now I know what it means. It means that you and I saw something beautiful together and we will always have that and now it is the only thing I have.... Hello...hello...please...someone....

CONSTANTIN: *(He enters slowly as though he was not sure that she was there.)* Anna?

ANNA: Huh? Who's there?

CONSTANTIN: It's me, Constantin.

ANNA: You better get out of here and tell your pimp friends I've got a gun and I don't care! I'll count to three! *(She pulls out a gun.)*

CONSTANTIN: Anna, it's not like that.

ANNA: One!

CONSTANTIN: You're making a mistake.

ANNA: Two! If you don't get out it will be you that is making the mistake!

CONSTANTIN: I love you, Anna.

ANNA: You work for them! You followed me and you work for them!

CONSTANTIN: No! I mean, yes! I did follow you. But I followed you because I love you.

ANNA: I don't believe you. It is too fantastic to believe. You speak like a Buddha but have a snake in your heart!

CONSTANTIN: I have come to take you home.

ANNA: Back? Back where? Siberia?

CONSTANTIN: I want to show you something.

ANNA: Why would I want to go back? I have come to America to dance. You can do anything you want in America and be happy too. See how well it has worked out for me. They tried to turn me into a prostitute. I like it. I'm very happy.

CONSTANTIN: I want to show you this picture.

ANNA: What picture?

CONSTANTIN: This photograph.

ANNA: What is it?

CONSTANTIN: Here. I'll show you.

ANNA: Don't come any closer. I'm still counting to three, you know. And I'm already on two!

CONSTANTIN: But I…

ANNA: Put it on the table there and step way back. *(He does what she says and she picks up the photograph and looks at it.)* So what? What about it?

CONSTANTIN: What do you think?

ANNA: I think you work for them and if you do not come clean and tell me straight out what you want I am going to finish counting.

246

CONSTANTIN: I want that to be yours—to be ours—together. Just tell me what you see in the photograph.

ANNA: A house. It's a cottage with decorations on it.

CONSTANTIN: What else?

ANNA: And there's ornaments and details all over this cottage with lines and vees and rope shapes and triangles and squares all in patterns and on the gate door there is a bright yellow sun with sun-rays and all these things are carved and painted green and yellow and brown and white and blue. It's a beautiful cottage.

CONSTANTIN: I mean it, Anna.

ANNA: You mean it?

CONSTANTIN: Yes.

ANNA: You mean what?

CONSTANTIN: It.

ANNA: What is it?

CONSTANTIN: That I have loved you since kindergarten. You loved to dance and that is a glamorous thing. You are an artist. All I ever wanted was to build things, my hands touching wood. I am not Mr. Romance. I'm just a fellow who can build cottages and who loves you. I came to watch you dance in the Actors Café. You were in trouble. I came to get you out of trouble because I love you. You do not

247

have to take my offer. You can have the cottage to yourself. Only come back with me.

ANNA: I don't know whether to believe you. It is too fantastic. My head is mixed up.

CONSTANTIN: Believe me because it is true.

ANNA: But if it is true what about dance? Dance means everything to me. I have to dance Constantin. I have to dance!

MAURA: (*Enters and sees the gun.*) Hey! Drop that gun!

ANNA: Who are you?

MAURA: This is my place and I say no guns allowed!

ANNA: Your place?

MAURA: My place! Drop that gun!

ANNA: You mean you don't work for them?

MAURA: I work for me and of course the United States government who takes much of what I earn even though I don't report all of it and if I did I'd be out of business anyhow so give me that gun!

ANNA: What?

CONSTANTIN: Give her the gun.

ANNA: No. I'm leaving. No one follow me, understand! I don't trust anyone. I trusted Dimitry.

CONSTANTIN: You know me Anna. Everything I have said is the truth.

ANNA: It is?

CONSTANTIN: It is.

MAURA: He's telling the truth.

ANNA: How do you know?

MAURA: Look at him. Look at that face. This guy is loaded with sincerity. Could that face lie? Look at it!

ANNA: I'm looking, I'm looking.

CONTANTIN: Anna....

ANNA: *(She hands the gun to Maura who throws it in the garbage.)* I'm in a terrible heck of a mess. I fall in love and want to dance and I end up lost.

MAURA: You want to dance?

ANNA: That's right.

MAURA: She wants to dance?

CONSTANTIN: That's what she wants.

MAURA: I'll give you a chance, kid. That's all anyone wants in this life, is a fighting chance.

ANNA: A chance?

MAURA: Sure. We got a little stage here and people come in and have a drink or two and you can dance and be like the entertainment. I'll have to try you out first. I mean I can't make any promises.

ANNA: Promises...

MAURA: I can promise that if you have *anything,* I'll give you a chance.

ANNA: Anything? A chance?

MAURA: That's what I said.

CONSTANTIN: Listen to me, Anna, I am going to tell you something very important. I am going to tell you something bigger than any chance

ANNA: Something important?

CONSTANTIN: Yes, and it is this. You can come back to Siberia with me and dance in our cottage. We can put the music on and you can dance all day. We can have children and you can dance holding them and then they will dance too. To dance, all you need is a floor and someone who loves you. I love you. I will give you a floor, will build you a stage and you can dance on it and our children will dance on it and this earth will fly through space with us on it dancing. And when we are dead what will matter is this; we loved each other; we had children we loved; and I built cottages and you danced.

MAURA: I can try you out, kid, but that was some offer.

ANNA: I must choose. Is that it?

MAURA: Go ahead. Let's see you dance.

CONSTANTIN: In our world you dance when you want to dance.

ANNA: I want to dance all the time and make up dances. It is in my bones and blood.

CONSTANTIN: I will build you a stage.

MAURA: Come on, kid. Go ahead. I'll give you a chance. The more I think about it, the more I like the idea.

ANNA: What is my choice? I must decided. It is between Siberia and this.

CONSTANTIN: It is between love and this. There is no choosing, Anna. You know what is important in this life.

ANNA: I do?

CONSTANTIN: You do.

ANNA: I do.

CONSTANTIN: Let's go home, Anna.

ANNA: Yes. If everything you say is true, Constantin, than I love you.

CONSTANTIN: It is true. (*They begin to exit.*)

ANNA: Wait a minute. I need to say it. I choose Siberia and I choose you because I believe you and because you are right and I will dance with our children and I will dance on the stage you build and I will dance in our cottage. Yes. I say *yes*, Constantin. I say yes to you. But I am afraid of Dimitry. We better go out the back door.

CONSTANTIN: No. We will go out the front door. I will take care of the Dimitrys of this world by loving you and you will take care of Dimitry by loving me.

ANNA: Good-bye, whoever you are. (*Anna and Constantin exit.*)

MAURA: Good-bye, kid! There they go. Gee, I really had my heart set on a dancer in the place. Say, why just one dancer?! I'll get a dance troupe in here. I can see it.! The Isadora Duncan Café! As a matter of fact, Isadora Duncan sat in that chair over there; that one over there. First thing tomorrow morning I'll put an ad in the paper for some dancers. The Iroquois Hotel is on the move! (*She turns to the audience.*) Well, I'm closing up, folks. Good-night. Drive carefully. And may God bless you.

(BLACK OUT)

The Day Frank Sinatra Died

A Comedy in Two Acts

By Dan Sklar

Dan Sklar

CHARACTERS

MAGGIE DUMONT	GARY MILLER
AMANDA DUMONT	FRANK COSTELLA
MAUREEN DUMONT	REGGIE
SIMONE DUMONT	JOE HENNESSE
AMELIA DUMONT	JIMMY MAHONEY

SETTING

The living room of the DuMont's who live in a mansion on East 81ˢᵗ Street in Manhattan. The home is well lived in with big old oak furniture that is at once tasteful and functional. There is an atmosphere of solid wealth without a hint of pretension.
The time is the present. It is early evening. Maggie, twenty-five, is in her pajamas and is seated on the floor. She is writing in a notebook and thinking out loud. This play is fast and physical.

MAGGIE: I am thinking about New York coffee shops. I like the sound of the word, Coffee. I like everything about coffee. Black coffee. Who knows the thing about   black coffee and a cigarette? Joe does. I think about Joe and me in a Lexington Avenue coffee shop on some snowy Tuesday afternoon. We sit by the window and don't say anything to each other because there is nothing more to say. We drink black coffee and smoke Old Gold cigarettes. We just finished talking about getting married and we have decided to do it. A man at the counter is talking in Spanish to the cook. A man comes in with his son. They sit at the counter and have malted milk shakes. A women is reading a thick paperback book as she drinks black coffee. Everything is

254

bright and gleaming stainless steel and glass. Two men in suits are talking about money and business deals. And me and Joe are sitting there wanting and knowing that we will get married and we decided to do it and we look into each others eyes.

AMELIA: (*Enters. She is in her early sixties. She wears a black evening gown with pearls.)* Maggie, honey. You are supposed to be getting dressed.

MAGGIE: In a minute mother. (*Going back to her notebook.)* A man sits at the counter and orders apple pie and a cup of coffee.

AMELIA: Now, Maggie! The boys will be here. We have reservations.

MAGGIE: They are always late, mother! I'm writing here. I'm on to something! Where are we eating? Two adolescent girls in a booth are eating vanilla ice cream. They both talk at the same time and laugh about everything. They do not know how free and happy they are. And now we feel free and happy—me and Joe. Joe. I think about Joe. Just a guy named Joe. How corny can you get? I like being corny. You have to get corny when you are getting married.

AMELIA: They won't be late tonight. The O. Henry.

MAGGIE: The O. Henry! Oh, thank you mother. I love the O. Henry room of the Iroquois Hotel. It's fitting and it's perfect and I'll tell you why.

AMELIA: It's wonderful to see you happy, Maggie.

MAGGIE: I am happy, mother. Just think. Two engagement parties. Has that ever happened before? Two sisters and one engagement party. Maureen and me. Frank proposed to her almost the same day that Joe and I decided. Isn't that amazing, mother! Oh, but when there is happiness, there has to be sadness too. Where is the sadness mother? I know. You don't have to tell me. My other two sisters, Amanda and Simone. No one has asked them to get married.

AMELIA: Don't worry about Amanda and Simone, Maggie. They are younger than you. They're time will come. They know that. They aren't sad.

MAGGIE: But what if it never comes? What if they never get married? Oh, I know they have those boyfriends, but what if something happens?

AMELIA: Just have fun tonight, dear. Jimmy is ambitious. The minute something breaks for him, he'll ask Simone. Now get dressed, honey.

MAGGIE: But suppose he doesn't? Suppose he gets a part in a play and gets famous and moves to Hollywood. He'll have all the girls he wants. He won't need Simone anymore. Oh, this is too much. His success can be the very thing that ruins them. I cannot bear thinking about it.

AMELIA: Maggie. Your driving yourself mad. You find things to worry about before you have to worry about them. Now go into your bedroom and get dressed.

MAGGIE: Yes. I'll get dressed. But what about Amanda? Do you think Gary will want to marry her? I mean he is so nice and all and she is so, you know, not nice and all and mean and…. Wait a minute. What if he wants to marry her for our money? Or worse, for Simone! That would be the dirtiest, rottenest thing… I think I want to stay in my pajamas. I'm comfortable.

AMELIA: Please, Maggie…. (*The doorbell rings.*) Reggie. The door.

REGGIE: (*Enters and goes to answer the door.*) Yes, ma'am.

MAGGIE: Oh, and Reggie, call me a taxi cab while you're at it.

REGGIE: A taxi, ma'am?

MAGGIE: Yes, a hack, a cab, a taxi, a checker cab. A taxi is poetry I tell you, don't you think? It's a poem, me, sitting in a cab in my pajamas. A taxi driver driving. Manhattan's poetry of the streets is the battalions of taxi cabs flying down 2nd Avenue at four A.M. Yes, instead of going to my engagement party, I'd like a cab to the airport and then get on a plane for Iceland. I want to go to Iceland and sit at the bar in some woody old Icelandic Tavern, and drink ice cold vodka. At first I want to be alone, but maybe later someone could talk to me. Get me a taxi, Reggie.

AMELIA: Answer the door, Reggie. Maggie, you come with me. *(Starts to lead her to her bedroom.)*

REGGIE: Shall I call a taxi cab, ma'am?

AMELIA: Of course not.

MAGGIE: Of course yes. I will meet you at the Iroquois Hotel, mother. I think I will get a room there. Yes. I will get dressed there. I will pack my bags. I need to pack some things in a small plaid suitcase; and it will be like a surprise. I've always wanted to stay in a hotel for no particular reason. That is poetry, don't you think? A women in a hotel room for no particular reason.... I...

AMANDA: *(Enters. She is twenty-one. She is in her bathrobe.)* Pipe down here, Maggie would you. How can anybody read the encyclopedia with all this racket?

MAGGIE: A strange, mysterious women, alone. Eating alone. What would I eat?

AMELIA: Amanda! You're not even dressed! We have eight-thirty reservations! Reggie, would you please open the door for Mr. Hennesse. And you two....

AMANDA: Dressed? For what?

MAAGGIE: Do you see that, mother? Amanda is not happy about this. Why must my happiness, my engagement, be her sadness.

AMANDA: Who said I was sad? What are you talking about?

AMELIA: Reggie, would you please let Mr. Hennesse in!

REGGIE: How do you know it's Mr. Hennesse, ma'am?

AMANDA: Engaged? What for? Who's engaged? Engaged to be what?

MAGGIE: It is I, I mean me, that is engaged. And our sister, Maureen. I am engaged aren't I mother? Engaged to be married?

AMANDA: Did I choose these sisters? Did I ask you to be my sister? No. We are stuck with our siblings and relatives whether we like it or not. I have to consider whether or not I like it. Besides, anybody even considering or thinking about getting married ought to have her head examined.

AMELIA: There is nothing for you to think or do but to get dressed. We are going out for the evening. Amanda, tonight is the night of the engagement party of your sisters. You would do well to go into your room and get ready. That is the right thing for you to do now.

JOE: (*Enters. He is a in his twenties. He wears an old baggy blue suite and tie and fedora had pulled down to his eyes. He needs a shave. He lights a cigarette before he speaks.*) Let myself in. Reggie. Drink.

REGGIE: Drinks, ma'am?

AMELIA: Yes. Cocktails are appropriate.

JOE: Beer. No glass. Can.

REGGIE: Yes, ma'am.

AMELIA: (*Extending her hand to Joe.*) Good evening, Mr. Hennesse. So good of you to come. Margaret was just about to get…

JOE: Dressed. How about if she gets undressed.

AMANDA: That was a witty crack.

MAGGIE: I wasn't going to do either. I was writing in my journal notebook. I'm working on a poem. Now that this living room is turning into Grand Pennsylvania Station, I will forthwith continue the poem in my bedroom. When I am writing a poem, nothing else matters.

JOE: She's writing a poem.

AMELIA: What are you going to do when you have children and they want you and you have to be with them, Maggie?

AMANDA: What do Buddhists do when they're meditating and their kids come around?

JOE: They yell at 'em all right and say, "Hey, get outta' here, can't ya see I'm meditating here." Lousy Buddhists.

AMANDA: Wait a minute. Don't tell me Maureen is marrying Frank Costella. He's got a white Cadillac. I mean a white Cadillac. Not cream colored or beige. White, for crying out loud. Have you ever seen how he turns and looks at it as he walks away from it. He sort of glances back at it. A big, fat white Cadillac. I hate how people look at their cars.

JOE: Where's Simone?

AMANDA: Simone, Simone, Simone!

GARY: *(Enters. He is in his twenties. He wears a pressed gray suit. He is clean cut.)* The door was open Mrs. DuMont, so I took the liberty to respectfully, aaaa, enter, that is come in. Oh, hello everyone. Hello, Amanda, I have something for you.

REGGIE: May I get you a drink, ma'am.

AMELIA: Good evening, Mr. Miller. You must excuse Margaret and Amanda, they were about to get ready.

GARY: Good evening, Mrs. DuMont. You look quite lovely this evening.

AMELIA: Thank you, Mr. Miller.

MAAGIE: How come you don't say things like that to my mother, Joe?

JOE: I don't say things like that.

GARY: These flowers are for you, Amanda.

AMELIA: Reggie, please get Gary a drink.

REGGIE: What would you like ma'am?

GARY: Martini, Reggie. Here, Amanda.

AMELIA: The flowers are lovely, Gary.

AMANDA: I don't want flowers. I don't want anything from you or anyone else. I don't want gifts, see, because gifts from you mean you want to get into my pants. Give them to Maggie here. Let her look at them and smell them and then write some stupid poem about. I hate poems about flowers. If I get another gift in my life it will be too soon. Give them to Simone; she loves flowers. She'll wear them round her head and make a crazy little skirt out of them, for Christsake.

MAGGIE: I wouldn't write a poem about flowers if you paid me. How come you don't bring me flowers or gifts or anything like that, Joe?

JOE: What for?

259

AMELIA: Girls, you may be excused to get ready for the evening. Maggie this is your engagement party too. Maureen has already taken a shower and is putting on her makeup. I wish you two could be a little bit like Maureen.

MAGGIE: I can get dressed in two minutes flat, mother. I don't need makeup or anything. Besides, I don't want flowers. I want chocolates or some kind of food. Celery. Bananas. Carrots. Food, is a meaningful and useful gift.

JOE: Someone's at the door. It's open.

AMELIA: Reggie, the door.

REGGIE: Yes, ma'am.

AMANDA: I have everything I need, and if I want something, I go and get it. I don't need people to give me gifts so I will think they like me and I will like them.

GARY: She's a kidder all right, a beautiful kidder.

MAGGIE: Kidder. I kid you not. Handle her with kid gloves. Kids. Are we going to have kids, Joe. I think I want kids. I'm not sure. But I don't want to regret not having kids. We have to think of the future. How many kids do we want? How are we going to let them shape happy lives? I want five children. I will stay home with them because they will be the most important people in the world to me.

JIMMY: *(Bolts on with energy and enthusiasm. He wears white pants and a blue sports jacket, a vest and bow tie, saddle shoes, and a straw boaters hat. He looks like he just stepped out of a dance number with Gene Kelly.)* Folks! Hold on to your hats because I am the man of the hour, the minute, the second. I am the man of now! Many are called, but I have been chosen! And you will ask of what circumstances I speak and why I am the man.

JOE: No we won't.

MAGGIE: Yes we will.

AMANDA: Who cares. I take one look at him and I don't care about anything. I'm hungry, mother. What's for dinner?

AMELIA: Gentlemen, please excuse Amanda. She hasn't found herself like the rest of my daughters. I have suggested she go to college to be a physical therapist. I read that that is the up and coming field. Or something to do with computers.

AMANDA: I'd rather be in a down and going field. Actually, I'd prefer a baseball field, alone, at night. No lights.

MAGGIE: What shall I eat at my engagement dinner? This is very important.

JIMMY: Mrs. DuMont, may I say you look ravishing this evening.

AMELIA: Hello, Mr. Mahoney. Yes you may.

MAGGIE: How come you never say I look ravishing, Joe?

JOE: I try not to say anything.

JIMMY: Where's Simone? I want her to hear it straight and right and directly from the horses hoof, I mean mouth.

AMELIA: Simone is getting dressed. It takes her hours. Would you like a cocktail, Jimmy?

GARY: I'll see what's keeping Simone.

JOE: No, I want to see.

AMELIA: Reggie, would you offer Mr. Mahoney a drink.

REGGIE: Yes ma'am. Would you like a drink, ma'am?

JIMMY: Scotch on the rocks. Make it the Chevas, Reggie.

REGGIE: Very good, ma'am.

JIMMY: Does she have to call me ma'am? I think that I should get Simone, considering the fact that she is my girlfriend and she ain't anybody else's.

MAGGIE: Don't leave this room. Simone comes in her own time. Nobody rushes Simone. There's no getting Simone. You can't tell Simone what to do.

AMELIA: Jimmy, must you use that word in this house? My dear departed late husband, Harris DuMont the third, would die if he wasn't already dead if he heard "ain't" uttered or otherwise spoken or said in this house. It's been two years since he died. He would be very happy today to see his girls grown up and having this engagement party. I like to think that somehow he is with us tonight. I would want him to be glad at how polite and cooperative and fine and generous his girls have become. With that in mind, shall we leave shortly for the O. Henry room at the Iroquois Hotel. We have eight-thirty reservations.

JOE: The O. Henry Room. O. Henry was a fine rummy. Swell.

MAGGIE: Yes, O. Henry. The question is, what shall we eat, Joe. This is our engagement party to be married dinner. I want to relish everything about it. It is important that I taste every bite of food and sip of drink. I will butter my bread with plenty of butter. I really like butter. Ever notice how little kids and old grandpas eat butter? They smooth it out in a dense thick solid sheet to the ends of the bread, and sometimes they shake salt on it. They think about eating butter right from the stick. I shall eat butter for the rest of my life.

JOE: Poetry.

MAGGIE: It is. It is.

GARY: We're not eating anything at the O. Henry if we don't get a move on, I think.

JIMMY: But before we pile into cabs and race down 5th Avenue, to the Iroquois, let me just spill this little news, this bit of informative information for your information, edification, and elucidation. I just gotta tell someone…

JOE: Why us?

AMANDA: I like you, Joe. We think alike, you and me. Yeah, Jimmy, save it for Simone. We don't want to be edified, informed, or elucidated. We don't want to know anything about you.

JIMMY: Just for that, I'm telling you anyhow.

MAGGIE: Tell us all about it, Jimmy, kid. Gives us the details too.

AMELIA: Yes, but please be concise.

JIMMY: Feast and lay your eyes ladies and gentlemen on Jimmy Mahoney! He dances, he sings, he does monologues, dialogues, catalogues, Shakespeare—you name it! And why am I so happy? I'll tell you why…

AMANDA: Mother, I'm going to my room. I'm staying home. I can't bear to hear about other people's successes. It's too emotional for me. Besides, I was just about to read Infinity to Katmai, book volume number thirteen of the *Collier's Encyclopedia.*

JOE: Who said anything about success?

MAGGIE: He must have gotten lucky. Success is luck, a little talent, but mostly, luck—a hell of a lot of luck. Sometimes it's all talent and no luck or no talent and all luck. Who knows? I know. No I don't.

AMANDA: Success is when you do something good and you get blue about it.

JOE: Success is when I really slam some hack city worker in the *Post Dispatch* and then that first sip of beer at the White Cat Pub, and the first drag of an Old Gold cigarette in the New York dusk.

MAGGIE: I had a poem published in the *New York Quarterly* once. It was the bluest moment of my life. It was a lousy poem.

JOE: It's better to be a miserable failure at something. Take me, I'm perfectly happy being a third rate hack reporter for a second rate newspaper. Hell, when your standards are low, you have plenty of them.

AMANDA: I think the search and quest and desire for happiness is a joke.

AMELIA: All I can say is it's a good thing you girls were born with silver spoons in your mouth. If you can't be happy when you're rich; you can't be happy at all.

MAGGIE: The trick is not to look for it. I desperately wanted to be published. Then I was so miserable, I stopped caring and it happened; and I had no excuse to be sad anymore. So I forced myself to be miserable. I'm much happier that way.

AMANDA: Our father is dead and we can never be happy.

AMELIA: Oh that's the silliest notion I ever heard. You have to choose happiness and take it. I certainly did. This is Maureen's engagement party, too. I want you all at least pretend to be happy. Act happy, damn it!

JIMMY: I don't have to pretend, Mrs. DuMont.

Dan Sklar

AMELIA: I know you don't, Jimmy.

GARY: Me neither. All I have to do is think things. For instance, I'm thinking about how maybe I ought to give those flowers to Simone. I'd like to see her in a skirt made out of flowers. Thinking about that makes me happy.

AMANDA: I hate that "for instance" stuff. You'd like to get under those flowers! You don't care who's wearing them.

GARY: I was joking. I want you to wear them, Amanda.

AMANDA: I get it, men give women flowers because secretly they want the women to take off their clothes and wear flowers.

JOE: Men give women flowers because they want them to take off their clothes.

AMELIA: Please, Mr. Hennesse! Jimmy, you were going to tell us something.

GARY: Yes, Jimmy, quick, lighten things up around here.

AMANDA: I'll darken things up, buddy! The only reason I go out with you is because I hate you so much—you and your young republican friends…. And if I wasn't so addicted to fresh chocolate nonpareils and peanuts, which I can only get from your crummy little nut store on Broadway, I'd never look at your ugly face again.

GARY: (*Laughs nervously.*) Ha, ha, ha. What a kidder.

AMANDA: I never kid.

JOE: She never kids.

MAGGIE: I hate poetry and I can't stop writing it and I'm a lousy poet. I suppose it is better to a bad poet than a bad doctor or something. At least I can't kill anyone by mistake.

JOE: Yeah, but you can make us suffer because we have to read it.

GARY: Don't let it get you down. You're young. You can improve. You should try rhyming, then you'll be a real poet.

AMANDA: Let it get you down, Maggie. You stink.

AMELIA: Mr. Mahoney, save us from these eternal stick-in-the-muds.

JIMMY: Gladly, Mrs. DuMont. But I'd kind of like for everyone in the party to hear this. It's sort of a double, no triple, celebration because, well, I was going to tell Simone first, so promise you won't say anything until I do. But, you know, all of this engagement stuff is pretty contagious…

AMANDA: Like a disease.

JIMMY: And before I tell you about what I did today, I want to show you this! *(He take a ring box from his vest pocket, opens it, and shows them a diamond engagement ring.)*

GARY: Is that for Simone?

AMELIA: Oh, Jimmy!

JOE: You think you can marry Simone?

AMANDA: That's a laugh. A real knee slapper. Now that is a joke, Gary. That's a funny joke.

JOE: Nobody marries Simone.

MAGGIE: What was the other thing you wanted to tell us?

AMANDA: Have you got an Alfa Romeo car?

JIMMY: No.

MAGGIE: You have to have an Alfa Romeo car.

AMANDA: Red. Convertible.

JIMMY: What?

MAGGIE: And you have to ride with the top down. Simone never gets cold.

JIMMY: What are you talking about?

AMANDA: For Simone to even think about marrying anyone, he would have to have an Alfa Romeo car. 1988.

MAGGIE: What's your other news?

JIMMY: I love Simone and she loves me.

JOE: That acting is really getting to your head, pal. You are living a little too truthfully in imaginary circumstances.

JIMMY: What imaginary circumstances?

AMANDA: You're a bigger idiot than I thought.

MAUREEN: *(Enters. She wears a long pale green satin evening gown. She has thick black hair and bright green eyes and pink cheeks. She holds her purse and is ready to go. She is lovely and glowing.)* Well, everybody, I am ready for one of the finest evening of my life. The evening I have dreamed about and longed for, my engagement to be married party. Has my knight in shining white Cadillac arrived?

AMELIA: Maureen, sweetheart. You are radiant. Isn't she beautiful, everyone.

GARY: Yeah, like an angel.

MAGGIE: A shining sharp star.

JOE: Where's Simone?

JIMMY: You make me jealous of Frank.

AMANDA: Pff.

MAUREEN: I cannot tell you all, all of you, how happy I am. But I will save the speeches for later in the evening of this enchanting and elegant time in our nubile lives. Yes, this is my magical, beautiful time. And I shall savor and cherish every moment of it.

MAGGIE: Me too.

AMANDA: I thought she was going to save the speeches.

MAUREEN: My perfect youth. My *jeunesse doree.* I am twenty-one. I am beautiful. I am beautiful. Dear, dear, mother; I am so, so happy.

AMELIA: That is exactly what a mother wants to hear. Thank you, Maureen. You are everything you say and feel you are. My beautiful daughter.

AMANDA: I am so, so nauseated.

MAGGIE: Hark! I hear a white Cadillac.

GARY: How can you tell it's white?

MAGGIE: Reggie, prepare to open the door.

MAUREEN: Now I shall go to my room. A woman must always keep a man waiting just enough, but not too much mind you, so that he thinks about her, imagines her, pictures her, and desires her. *(She exits.)*

JOE: But everyone wants Simone.

AMANDA: Boyfriends probably wouldn't stick around for long if it wasn't for Simone; which I don't even want a boyfriend in fact.

GARY: She's a laugh riot, that Amanda. What a sense of humor.

AMANDA: I don't have a sense of humor.

JOE: Maybe not exactly a laugh riot.

AMELIA: Amanda! Margaret! To your rooms now! I'm not having you ruin this night for Maureen.

AMANDA: She'll never notice.

MAGGIE: You know you're right, mother. We must let Maureen have this night too. I must include Maureen in my poem. I must put Simone and Amanda and mother and every person that I love and loves me. And I will recite this poem this evening in the O. Henry room of the Iroquois Hotel.

GARY: Will the poem rhyme?

JOE: Poems that rhyme, suck; even Shakespeare.

MAGGIE: If I write a poem and rhymes coincidentally crop up; I cut them. It's fantastic how much I hate rhyming poetry, even good rhyming poems. Just thinking about it makes me want to throw up. Let me tell you something, Gary, I took creative writing in college and of the seventy-nine forms of poetry, eighteen use a rhyming scheme device. That's less that one quarter! And every two-bit idiot like you thinks that poetry has to rhyme! I can't bear to think about some poet sitting around trying to find words that rhyme. Oh! I can't go on! *(She exits dramatically.)*

JOE: There she goes.

JIMMY: I wonder what she really feels about rhyming poetry?

AMELIA: Amanda!

AMANDA: What?

AMELIA: What do you think?

AMANDA: But I need a dramatic exit line

AMELIA: Think of one and then exit.

AMANDA: Gimme those flowers. I'm going to wear a dress of flowers. Yes. I will be a girlie girl tonight. Nothing but flowers. I do so, so love flowers... *(She exits as dramatically as Maggie.)*

267

JOE: This is some family.

AMELIA: Now, gentlemen. As for you, maintain your dignity this evening. As you know my daughters are oddly articulate. They say too much of what they think and feel, which I suppose is better than suicide, but it makes people nervous. It is up to you boys to see that things go smoothly and no one gets embarrassed.

GARY: How are we supposed to do that, Mrs. DuMont?

AMELIA: Put your napkins in your lap, chew with your mouth closed, dip the soup spoon in away from you, break your bread into small pieces, say charming and and witty and fine and positive things only. Is that clear?

JOE, GARY, JIMMY: Yes, Mrs. Dumont.

AMELIA: Very good. Reggie, take care of these gentlemen. *(She exits.)*

REGGIE: Yes, Ms. DuMont. Refills, boys?

GARY: Don't bother, Reggie. *(He and Jimmy race to the bar.)*

JIMMY: We'll help ourselves.

JOE: A.O.K. beer, Reggie.

REGGIE: A.O.K. beer, ma'am?

JOE: Any Old Kind.

FRANK: *(Enters quietly and moves gracefully like a cat. He surveys the room with his eyes. He has no expression on his face. He looks back out the at his Cadillac. He wears a double-breasted suit. His hair is slicked straight back. He leans against the doorjamb and steadily flips a quarter up and catches it like a George Raft character. He does not speak yet.)*

GARY: Let me be the first to congratulate you, Frank. You're a mighty lucky guy.

JIMMY: Maureen's a great girl. She wants all the right things.

JOE: She's Simone's sister; that's the important thing, right?

FRANK: Thanks, boys.

REGGIE: Drink, Mr. Costella?

FRANK: Scotch.

REGGIE: Very good, sir.

FRANK: Where's Simone?

JIMMY: How come she doesn't call him ma'am? I like the way he says, Very good, sir. If I ever play a butler, which I won't, that's how I'll say that line. But, boys, let me tell you, I just got the plum part of a lifetime—the kind of role every actor worth anything dreams about. I got it.

JOE: Leave it outside.

GARY: What is it, Jim?

JIMMY: You fellas ever read a little classic type novel called *The Last of the Mohicans*?

JOE: Yeah.

GARY: I saw the movie. I was supposed to read it in college. I read some of the Cliff Notes. I just listened in class; not much, but a little. I still got B on the paper. Idiot professors.

JIMMY: I'll tell you guys, but don't say anything. This is Maureen's and Maggie's night, not mine. Okay. This is it. You, my fine feathered friends, are looking at Natty Bumppo—otherwise known as Hawkeye, the trapper, scout—in the new Broadway Musical Play, *The Last of the Mohicans.*

GARY: Musical!?

JIMMY: That's right.

JOE: You mean you dance and sing?

JIMMY: Yep.

JOE: I think I'm going to kill myself.

GARY: You mean they're making *The Last of the Mohicans* into a musical show?

JIMMY: Ubet they are, and I are, I mean, I am in it. I get to wear that raccoon hat and those deerskin trousers and shirt with the fringes and all; and I carry a musket and that horn thing for the gunpowder....

JOE: *The Last of the Mohicans,* a musical for Christ's sake.

FRANK: Good for you, kid. But it's a dirty shame they have to bump off a decent adventure story like that.

JOE: Next thing you know, they'll do that to *Treasure of Sierra Madre,* for crying out loud.

JIMMY: What are you guys talking about?

JOE: Nothing.

FRANK: *The Old Man and the Sea.* A musical. Hemingway. The song will be "Fish, I love you and I hate you, fish."

JOE: The musical: *Of Mice and Men.* Steinbeck. They sing, "'George, tell me about the rabbits, George.' I already told you about the rabbits, Lenny!'" That'd be a swell song.

FRANK: *Moby Dick.*

JIMMY: Hey, this part is as manly as manly can be! I am a man's man in this thing, see! I'm talking about waterfalls right there on stage, horses, birch bark canoes, men running, hand to hand combat, tomahawks, knives, arrows, woods, forests primeval, wilderness, French spies, soldiers in uniforms, forts, Indians, canoes, sweat, kissing women in the dirt, rocks, meadows, Iroquois, Mohicans, Hurons, rocks, trees, shooting deer and eating them!

JOE: Okay, but do you have to dance and sing about it?

GARY: That's what the people want.

JOE: The people are idiots. They laugh at clichés and dirty words.

JIMMY: That is not my concern. I am an actor—an artist. What's important to me is that I get to say great lines like, "To eat we must find game. Speak of the devil, the biggest antlers I have seen this season are moving in those bushes on the hill. Uncas, take your bow and kill that buck for our dinner." And, "In the wilderness, saving a friends life is an obligation. Why, Sagamore has stood between me and death five times that I can remember. We must die as bravely as we fight." And, "Let him go. He is separated from his French friends. He has no rifle. He is as harmless as a rattlesnake who has lost his fangs." And, "The colors of our skin may be different, but God has placed us on the same path." You see, that's what it is about being an actor, you get to say great lines, and then go home.

GARY: There you go. The cream rises to the top. Talent wins out, eventually. Jimmy has been at this acting racket and it finally pays off. Next stop, Hollywood.

JIMMY: And I'm taking Simone with me. Here's the punch line of the story, boys, my agent has the Hollywood thing in the works, and pals, I ain't leaving this town without Simone.

FRANK: You actually think she will leave Manhattan?

JIMMY: I'm gonna get me a red convertible Alfa Romeo car. Drive it with the top down no matter what. Simone will come.

GARY: Oh she'll come all right, but it's not going to be in California.

JIMMY: Very funny. What's keeping Simone, anyway. I'm going up to see her.

(*He starts to exit but stops as Amelia enters.*)

AMELIA: Mr. Costella. Frank. So good to see you. I am very happy. How is your mother? I'm so sorry she won't be joining us.

FRANK: You're looking lovelier than ever, Mrs. DuMont. I am sure that Maureen will always be as charming and beautiful as you. My dad used to say, son, look at the mother, that's how the daughter will turn out

AMELIA: Thank you, Mr. Costella. We'll all have another cocktail, Reggie, and then call us two taxis cabs

REGGIE: Yes, ma'am, Ms. DuMont.

MAGGIE: (*Enters still wearing her pajamas.*) Frank! How's the white Cadillac?

AMELIA: Margaret!

MAGGIE: I'd like to drive to some roadhouse tavern type place, way out in New Jersey. Yes. Some place in the woods. Some crummy rotten dive of a place with stuffed deer heads and moose heads on the wall and snow shoes and crap like that.   And everything you get there is loaded with mayonnaise. We can drink beer and eat things with plenty of mayonnaise in it. What do you say?

AMELIA: You all must excuse, Maggie. Please, she's not herself today. After all, it isn't every day one has an engagement party.

GARY: Only every six months or so. Right, Joe? Joe's used to this.

AMELIA: Rather warm weather we've been having lately, Don't you think, Mr. Costella.

MAGGIE: The opera. Let's all go to the opera and buy season tickets. And get dressed up and go to the opera. Puccini. I feel like listening to songs that make me cry.

JOE: Hey, what did one mink say to the other mink on the way to the slaughter?

GARY: This is a joke, right?

AMELIA: Come with me, Maggie, Amanda!

MAGGIE: No, mother. I want to hear the joke. You mean the minks are killed and then skinned and meet again at the opera?

JOE: Yeah, that's what I mean. They kill them and then skin them; right there in some building some place, right now maybe even. Then they meet dead, at the opera.

AMELIA: Is this supposed to be some kind of metaphorical point on getting engaged and then married.

GARY: That's a funny joke. The minks' last words are, see you at the opera. You know what you ought to do, Joe? Write a crime novel, a mystery. You should write those spy type intrigue novels with women with big tits with a guy in a tuxedo looking at them. People actually buy those books. You have to write about criminals or rich tycoons or rich women and poor handsome guys and sex addicts and adultery and infidelity and rotten things and dirty secrets that happen in peoples' families and all that. That's what the people want. You know what I love?

JOE: No.

GARY: Gangster type mob mobster Mafia books. That's how you can make money Anything to do with hit men and torpedo men with heaters and rods and suits and hats and hot head Italian lover types and all that. You know, like *The Godfather*. A guy gets half his head shot off in front of Umberto's Clam House, cigar still in his mouth! That's what I like to read about.

JOE: Why would I want to do that?

GARY: It's pretty obvious, isn't it?

JOE: No.

GARY: Come on.

JOE: Come on what?

GARY: Look at her? Every time it's something with Maggie.

JOE: Something what?

MAGGIE: Yes. What are you talking about? This is the evening of my engagement party.

AMELIA: May I please speak to you a moment, Maggie?

AMANDA: *(Enters and is also still in her bathrobe.)* The fact of the matter is, I have been reading about this women who lived on Montauk Point beach during World War II, and her job was to scan the horizon for Nazi ships and submarines and spies. She sat out on her deck with her binoculars and her martinis. The fact of the matter is there was an enemy. You could tell who the bad guy was. I need an enemy to fight. I need to be useful that way. Alone and useful. That's what I want. Yes. I figured it out. Alone and useful at the same time. That's the ideal life for me.

GARY: Nights can get pretty cold and lonely without someone.

AMELIA: Forget yourself for one night. It is nights like these, these important evenings that we must focus on our happiness. There is always some happiness. This is an evening for dreaming, for living in a sweet dream. You must become angels tonight. That's it. I want you both to go into your rooms and become angels like your sisters Maureen and Simone. Why not become angels tonight, and make our own heaven.

AMANDA: Okay, okay, mother, we'll become angels, but first there's just a couple of things I want to get straight before we make this heaven, before you spring for a fancy meal with five waiters hanging around the table and you give Frank and Joe very solid gold pocket watches. There's one thing I want to know from you, Mr. Costella.

AMELIA: Amanda!

MAGGIE: It's all right, mother, she knows what she's doing.

AMELIA: That's what I'm afraid of.

AMANDA: No one is making a chump out of my sister or me or anyone else in this family. I have got to be sure, positive, no question in my mind about something.

AMELIA: Frank and Maureen are engaged. Maureen will be out here any second now. That is all you or anyone else needs to know.

MAGGIE: So what? Big deal! People get engaged and unengaged every minute of the day. Look at me and Joe. How many times have we been engaged and unengaged?

JOE: I don't know.

MAGGIE: Sixteen, maybe seventeen times. We like it that way. It keeps the romance going. This way the great feeling of it lasts.

AMELIA: This is not the time or place to talk about these things.

MAGGIE: Sure it is, mother. I'm talking about the truth. Any time is good for that.

FRANK: It's all right, Mrs. DuMont. Maggie can say anything she likes.

AMELIA: That's the problem.

AMANDA: She don't have to do nothing. I'll say it. How's the thug business, Frank? How are the kickbacks and payoffs? How's the white Cadillac? How are the dirty back room deals? Contracting business, right? You'll provide well for our little Maureen, not that she needs being provided for well. This family could use a jolt of fresh blood. Maureen wants plenty of kids, a nice place on Long Island—the whole middle-class nine yards—because this idle rich upper-class life don't suit her like it suits the rest of us. And it suits the rest of us just fine.

AMELIA: Must you speak like someone from the street?

AMANDA: I must. Ask Joe about Mr. Costella. He's done a little investigative reporting.

AMELIA: Never mind her, Frank. Maureen and you and I and Jimmy and Simone will go to the O. Henry Room of the Iroquois Hotel ourselves. We must not ruin this evening for Maureen. Believe me, I love my daughters deeply, but they are somewhat…

GARY: Crazy.

AMELIA: Eccentric. I was going to say eccentric and young and outspoken. No one doubts your motives for a moment, Mr. Costella.

AMANDA: Are you kidding, I doubt his motives. I doubt everyone's dirty little motives.

REGGIE: Taxi cabs are waiting, Mrs. DuMont, ma'am.

JIMMY: Good. Cabs are here. We can continue this interesting, fascinating conversation at the O. Henry Room, what do you say everybody? Throw on some clothes, kids. I'll run upstairs and get Simone, and we'll be off into the night. The night is ours! Let's live it! "It is time to move out! Our truce with the Iroquois has come to an end." *(Starts to exit.)*

AMANDA: What the hell is he talking about?

MAGGIE: Wait a minute Jimmy. Actually I'd like to write a play about a pizza place, Tony's Pizza, where all they have is pizza and beer, see. Plain pizzas and bottles of Pabst Blue Ribbon Beer—nothing else. A few booths, a couple of tables, empty pizza boxes stacked by the window. No sign out front. Either you know about it or you don't. It's open when it's open. And the play will be people coming in and ordering pizzas and bottles of Pabst Blue Ribbon Beer.

JIMMY: Sounds terrific.

JOE: I like the beer part.

MAGGIE: Don't you get it, Jimmy? You know about theater and drama and all that. You could be one of the fellas that comes in, you see, and orders a slice of pizza and a beer.

FRANK: I'm a construction estimator. I live in Corona, Queens, with my mother. My uncle Angelo runs Costella Dante Construction Management Corporation. I work for my uncle estimating costs of materials and labor and time. I also do this for three other concerns. Mrs. DuMont, I love Maureen and she loves me. This is our engagement party.

AMELIA: Of course, Frank.

AMANDA: If we weren't so rich and Simone wasn't so beautiful, none of these boys would be here. If it wasn't for our great grandpa, McGrady DuMont, do you think Maggie here could be a poet? Not on your life!

MAGGIE: Writing is the thing that every cell in my body tells me to do. Thanks to McGrady DuMont it doesn't matter whether I am any good at it. When you're rich, who cares. *Tony's Pizza.* That's what I'll call it. I'm going to start writing it now! Tony's Pizza. No, Tony's famous pizza. *(She takes out her notebook and begins writing.)*

GARY: I thought you were a poet.

MAGGIE: A poet can write a play or anything else for that matter? It's all words. What's the difference? There is no difference. Everything is words. I love the word rugged. And that's the kind of people I like, rugged people. People who look you straight in the eye and say, I am rugged.

AMELIA: Here we go again. Send the cabs away, Reggie.

REGGIE: Very good, sir. Shall I pour more drinks.

JOE: You bet you shall, Reggie.

FRANK: When I met Maureen skiing up at Redtree Mountain, it was her shape and her eyes and her mouth that smiled in the cold snowy air that first attracted me.

AMANDA: Was this before or after you found out she was a DuMont?

FRANK: When I found out she was a DuMont, it was as if I had found out she had won medals for swimming, I was delighted. But let me tell you something…

AMANDA: Yeah, yeah. The next thing you're going to tell us you ain't marrying Maureen for her money. You're good, really good. What, did you go to charm school or something?

JIMMY: He comes by it naturally. Look, I'm going up for Simone. Wait a minute, but first listen to this one: "The laws of the white men mean nothing to the Iroquois. They are rules to a child's game." Simone! It is I, me, Natty Bumppo, Hawkeye, trapper from the forest, the woods where there is no corruption, only life and death."

MAGGIE: Life and death! I like it. I want things to be a matter of life and death. Tony's Famous Pizza. Our motto: It's a matter of life and death!

JIMMY: Alfa Romeo? Is that right?

AMANDA: That's right. Red Alfa Romeo. Top down no matter what.

MAGGIE: There's one other thing about it

JOE, GARY, JIMMY (*All together.*) What?

MAGGIE: What's all that Natty Bumppo forest white man Iroquois stuff about? One time I got lost in the woods. I took off my clothes and sat in the leaves. I think it is good to be alone and naked in the woods.

JOE: If you're naked in the woods does it make a sound?

AMELIA: This is a thoroughly fascinating conversation, children, however...Reggie, may I have a martini, please. Never mind, I'll make it myself.

REGGIE: Allow me, Ms. DuMont.

AMELIA : You put too much vermouth in. The way to make a good martini, Reggie is as you are mixing it you *think* about putting vermouth in, you never actually do it.

AMANDA: Kind of like the way it is with Simone, boys, you *think* about it, you never actually do it.

JIMMY: Hey, what's that crack supposed to mean?

REGGIE: Is there anything else, ma'am, Ms. DuMont, sir?

AMELIA: Anything else, why should there be anything else?

REGGIE: Shall I call two taxi cabs, sir?

GARY: Why would you want to call to taxi cabs, *sir?*

AMELIA: That will be all, Reggie.

REGGIE: That will be all of what, sir?

AMELIA: You may go now.

REGGIE: Go where?

AMELIA: Please, Reggie!

REGGIE: Don't give up, sir. You mustn't give up, even if appears it to be hopeless.

AMELIA: I am not giving up. I never throw in the towel, so to speak. I merely happen to be taking a brief hiatus from the battle. This evening will be a success, Reggie, you mark my words. This is a hiatus, that is all. I'll be back in the battle as soon as I finish this martini.

REGGIE: Very good, sir, ma'am, Ms. DuMont. Then I will be on hand to call the taxi cabs.

AMELIA: Thank you, Reggie.

REGGIE: You are quite welcome, sir, ma'am, Mrs. DuMont, sir.

MAUREEN: *(Enters and lights up the room.)* I am here mother.

FRANK: Maureen…

MAUREEN: Frank…

FRANK: Maureen…

MAUREEN: Frank…

AMANDA: Hey, you haven't told us what all that life and death and woods and trapper crap is? Not that I care, but maybe everyone else wants to know. Not that I care what everyone else wants. Not that I care about anything. I'm more interested in the principal method for making steel in the United States.

GARY: Jimmy got the part of Hawkeye in the new Broadway musical, *The Last of the Mohicans.* Isn't that wonderful?

JOE: Hell, it doesn't matter that they made it into a musical, the only thing good about that book was the title anyway.

AMELIA: Why, Jimmy, that is marvelous. Congratulations.

JIMMY: Thank you Mrs. DuMont. Incidentally, I don't want to blow my own horn or anything, but I never took an acting class in my life. I do what Jimmy Cagney, who I happen to

278

be named after said. In acting "you stand on the balls of your feet and tell the truth ."

AMELIA: We are all delighted for you ,Jimmy.

JIMMY: Thanks Mrs. Dumont. Say where is Simone? Do you know what room she is in now?

JOE: I figured out what bugs me about it. It's the fact that a couple of guys were sitting around some dopey pink grand piano in a Park Avenue place making up songs and dances about Hawkeye and Mohicans and Iroquois. Nobody's messing up my images if it! You ought to refuse to do it on the principle of the thing!

MAGGIE: *The Last of the Mohicans.* The last of anything is good, you know. I want to be the last of something. Romance is being the last. A last kiss before I die. If I was a Mohican I would want to be the last one. I always wait to be last on line. I sit in the last row in the theater, and I always sat in the back row in school. Last words. I wonder what my last words will be before I die? Robert E. Lee's last words were "Strike the tents." Emily Dickinson's last words were, "Called back." She was reading a novel called "Called Back." I wrote this poem once about how you can't really directly touch the thing you love, you can get near it, to the edge of it, all around it, every place about it, but not directly on it until... It's like Simone.

MAUREEN: Frank and I are ready, mother. Shall we meet you at the O. Henry ?

AMELIA: Just a moment, Maureen. I'm almost finished with my cocktail.

MAUREEN: But I am ready now, mother.

FRANK: That's all right, Maureen. Let your mother finish her drink.

MAUREEN: Yes, but that is not in my plan. I have a plan you see, and mother finishing her drink is not part of it.

GARY: What about Amanda and Maggie in their pajamas? Is that part of your plan?

MAUREEN: Mother!

279

AMELIA: Yes, dear?

FRANK: Don't think about it, kid. Everything's going to be just perfect.

MAUREEN: Will it, Frank?

FRANK: Yes, I'm telling you it will.

MAUREEN: Tell me how, Frank. Tell me how it's going to be right.

FRANK: I'll tell you. We're going to have this wonderful engagement dinner. Then in September, when it is cool and blue, we'll get married in an old ballroom with cool swing music and sweet music and candles on every table.

MAUREEN: Yes. What else, Frank?

FRANK: I'm telling you. We go for a honeymoon in a cabin in the woods with a fire in the fireplace and…. Then we move into our house right on the cliffs in Cliffside that overlooks the water. We'll have kids and love them and love each other and every day there will be romance between you and me—and every night.

MAUREEN: What else, Frank?

FRANK: What else is there, Maureen. Nothing else.

MAUREEN: You are right. There is nothing else. Reggie, you may get us a taxi, please. Frank and I are ready.

FRANK: Yes.

MAUREEN: Yes.

AMANDA: Poetry.

MAGGIE: Do I believe it?

JOE: Who asked you.

GARY: You have to believe it.

AMANDA: I don't believe anything.

AMELIA: I am through with my martini. You can believe it! *(She stands up and grabs Amanda and Maggie by their ear and starts to drag them out.)* Maureen! You come with us. You dress Maggie and I'll dress Amanda! I am the boss of this family and we are going to the O. Henry Room together! There has to be one boss and that boss is I—me! *(They exit.)*

MAUREEN: Yes, mother. Good-bye, Frank.

FRANK: Good-bye, darling. *(Maureen exits.)* There she goes.

JIMMY: Pardon me, boys. *(He starts to exit.)*

JOE: Where are you going?

JIMMY: You talking to me?

GARY: Nobody leaves this room.

FRANK: Scotch, Reggie.

JIMMY: Reggie, do you happen to know if Simone is in her room?

JOE: Beer.

REGGIE: Simone?

FRANK: Simone....

JOE: Simone...

JIMMY: Where is she?

JOE: Is she in the library?

GARY: Yeah, yeah, the library.

JIMMY: What do you care where Simone is?

GARY: Are you kidding, pal?

JIMMY: No, I'm not kidding, pal! I don't like you thinking and talking about her.

FRANK: Is that so?

JIMMY: Yes, that's so. And another thing…Say, what was that other thing she wanted beside the Red Alfa Romeo?

GARY: Red *1988* Alfa Romeo.

JIMMY: I don't want you even looking at Simone. l988?

JOE: 1988.

FRANK: Top down no matter what. But there was something else.... What was the other thing?

JIMMY: Shut up about Simone! I'm going to find her. *(Starts to exit. They all stop him.)*

FRANK: Where do you think you're going?

JIMMY: Find Simone. What's it to you?

JOE: You think you can find Simone? How long have you known Simone?

GARY: Simone could be anywhere in this mansion.

JIMMY: I'll find her.

FRANK: Everybody wants Simone.

Dan Sklar

REGGIE: Shall I ring for Simone, ma'am, sir?

JOE: And while you're at it, Reggie, we'll have more drinks.

GARY: And while you're at it, where is she?

JOE: Reggie ain't going to tell you where Simone is; you have to find her.

GARY: And then what? Does she actually sleep anywhere but in a dream?

JIMMY: What do you mean and then what?

GARY: What are you supposed to do when you find Simone?

JIMMY: This is getting too weird for me.

FRANK: You do what Jimmy here is doing, give Simone a ring.

JOE: You have to give Simone something.

GARY: What about the Alfa thing?

JOE: You don't want to blow it because of the Alfa thing.

FRANK: You don't want to take a chance, buddy. If she says no to you you're through, washed up, finished. There's no come back when they say no because they get into the habit of saying no. You have to get them in the habit of saying yes. If she says no because of the Alfa thing....Well, you ain't never gonna get Simone.

JIMMY: Maybe you're right.

FRANK: I know women. I'm right.

JIMMY: I have to find out what that other thing is.

AMELIA: *(Enters looking pleased and confident.)* Gentlemen. You may go to the study on the third floor. I will meet you there. I have a few things to say to you. I am going to play the role of Mr. DuMont, my late departed husband. Up and out, gentlemen!

JIMMY: Mrs. DuMont. You know how, Simone is and that Alfa Romeo thing and, and I ...I was wondering if you could explain about... 1988, red and all and, the other thing....

AMELIA: Mr. Costella. Mr. Hennesse, Mr. Miller, and Mr. Mahoney. Upstairs. Now!

JIMMY, JOE, FRANK, GARY: Yes, Mrs. DuMont. *(They exit.)*

AMELIA: Reggie?

REGGIE: Yes, Mrs. DuMont, sir. *(Reggie follows them out.)*

(Joe comes back for his cigarettes and when Simone enters from the other side he stays hidden to watch her. She does not know he is there. She is a voluptuary. She wears lion skins like Jane in the Tarzan movies. She seems to glow from within. She has flowers in her hair and stuck in her lion skin bikini. The air seems to boil around her. She holds a flower and when she talks she sometimes talks to it. She moves gracefully like a wild animal. She finds the flowers left behind and appears to make love to them as she tucks them into her clothing .

SIMONE: I have never been touched by a man. Men cannot get close enough. They do not make it. Men look at me and they cannot get me out of their head. I become what they imagine, you see. Men think about me when they make love to other women. Yes. I am an voluptuary. I am voluptuous. I have heard people say, she is voluptuous. They mean me. When men see me they are never the same. Their women notice their men suddenly become vigorous lovers. Yes, that's what I said; with me in their head they become vigorous lovers. I am the earth; the ground; the mud. These flowers will not die as long as they are touching me. Here I am in this Manhattan mansion and I am a danger to society. When I walk down the street I cause car crashes. I must go out only at night. My mother wants me to be a dentist. I am a goddess. A love goddess. How can a love goddess be a dentist? I sneak out of the house at dusk. I go to the park and twine twigs and leaves to make clothing. I cannot wear regular clothes. Somehow clothing does not want to stay on me. How do you dress a goddess? I move in my father's old overcoat, his hat pulled down over my eyes, along the buildings. I go to the theater. I sit in the mezzanine—alone. I go to restaurants and sit away from people—I eat alone. And men are thinking about me every minute of the day. I wander through this house. I wear my animal skins. They are the only thing my skin will tolerate. If a man ever touched my skin, he would die happy. I eat nuts and berries and grapes. I cannot wear jewelry or ornaments. I met this boy once—I saw him in a play downtown. He was a World War I soldier trapped in the trenches. Thirsty, hungry, wounded, shot in the leg. Dirt on his face, in his wounds. Sweating, coughing. He tore his shirt to tie around his leg. I fell in love with that wounded soldier, and in my mind I knew I loved him because he was wounded and he was a soldier. He longed for it to rain. The sun beat on him. He suffered so. I waited outside the stage door for the young wounded soldier. His name was Jimmy. He has come here tonight, but I am restless and wild. He will have to find me. I need to get away from this artificial light. Sunlight is the only light I can bear. But for now I will move in the shadows. *(She speaks to herself as she exits.)* Oh, where is my beautiful wounded soldier? I want to hold him. I want to hold him...

JOE: *(Has been staring at her. He watches her go. After she has gone he takes one of the drinks and splashes it in his face to cool himself off.)* Simone!

CURTAIN

ACT TWO

(The act opens with Joe still standing there in shock.)

JIMMY: *(Enters.)* Hey, Joe. Mrs. DuMont won't start talking until you get there. Joe. Joe, gimme a cigarette, would you. Joe, what's the matter?

JOE: Huh?

JIMMY: I said give me a cigarette?

JOE: Yeah, sure. Here.

JIMMY: Thanks. What's the matter with you?

JOE: Say, how long have you...I mean what do you do when you go out with her?

JIMMY: With who?

JOE: Who do you think?

JIMMY: Simone? (*Thinking about her.*) Ah, Simone....

JOE: *(Thinking about Simone.)* Yeah, I know what you mean.

JIMMY: No you don't.

JOE: I do. But what do you do with her?

JIMMY: She meets me after the show. I play Johnny Lewis in the World War I drama, *Blue Evening*. Have you seen it yet? I get wounded, it's great, my leg; and I'm stuck in this trench, see, starving and bleeding and thirsty and.... I'm bleeding to death I tell you, and every night I feel it too, what it's like bleeding to death, I mean. It's good.

JOE: Yeah, yeah, yeah, but what about Simone? What does she talk about, what does she think? Where do you take her? Level with me.

JIMMY: Why should I level with you?

JOE: Why do you think?

JIMMY: I don't *think*, I act. Thinking is the great enemy of art.

JOE: Use your head. You want to know that other thing Simone wants, right?

JIMMY: Right. The other thing.

JOE: Maybe I know.

JIMMY: You don't know. Say, she's been here, hasn't she? You saw her didn't you? I should have guessed from your stupid expression when I came in.

REGGIE: *(Enters.)* Pardon me, gentlemen, your presence is required in the study.

JOE: Required! Sounds like wired. Barbed wired! Would you like a cigarette, Reggie?

REGGIE: No thank you, ma'am.

JIMMY: Have a drink with us, Reggie, let your hair down. What do you say?

JOE: We just don't know you, Reggie.

JIMMY: That's right, and you seem like one of the family. And me and Joe here might be marrying into it.

REGGIE: Shall I pour more drinks?

JOE: Sure, and have one yourself.

JIMMY: Where are you from, Reggie, and how did you get into this maid type business?

REGGIE: Mrs. DuMont is waiting.

JOE: Forget Mrs. DuMont for two seconds would you? We want to find out about you.

JIMMY: You worry us, kid.

JOE: Yeah, you worry us, kid.

REGGIE: I worry you, kid.

JIMMY: Have a drink with us.

REGGIE: Well…

JOE: Come on, Reggie. For old times sake.

REGGIE: What old times, sir?

JOE: Here, I'll make *you* a drink for a change.

REGGIE: Thank you, ma'am.

JOE: Cigarette?

REGGIE: No, thank you.

JOE: Go ahead, have a cigarette.

REGGIE: I don't smoke, sir.

JIMMY: Take it up.

REGGIE: Shall I hail a taxi cab for you?

JOE: Characters, eh, Jimmy?

JIMMY: Characters.

JOE: Some family!

JIMMY: What a family!

REGGIE: I must clean up these drinks. Mrs. DuMont is in the study, so if you don't mind…

JOE: We don't mind. Sit down, Reggie. Have another drink.

JIMMY: I mean, that Simone!

JOE: That Simone. I'd like to write about her. Yeah, that's it, I'd like to write an article about the DuMonts for my paper, you know, the "New York Post Dispatch." Yes, an article, only in a favorable light, on what it's like to be rich. And I'd like some background on you, too, you know the loyal maid and all that. How long have you worked for the DuMont's?

REGGIE: Another can of beer, sir? Shall I draw your bath, ma'am.

JIMMY: She won't talk!

GARY: Mrs. DuMont wants you in the study on the double. Say, what is this?

JOE: Shut up. Give her a chance.

JIMMY: Look, you, I'm through playing games! I am going to give Simone this ring and I know she wants an Alfa Romeo car, red, 1988, top down know matter what; but there was one other thing about it that if I knew, it would cinch this for me, and you're going to spill it, see! Hey, that was pretty good. I really felt like a gangster. How did it sound? I really felt that. It was good.

GARY: Wait a minute, Reggie! We can make it worth you're while.

JOE: You stay out of this!

GARY: Get Frank, he'll know how to make her talk.

REGGIE: Good evening, gentlemen. I shall I bring you a cocktail.

JIMMY: Double-talk! Oh, that was good. I love saying things like, *double-talk*!

MAGGIE: *(Enters. She is dressed in wild colors like a Bohemian. She has on a red beret. She comes on determined.)* Joe. I figured it out. I thought it over and I've got it, Joe.

JOE: Got what? Thought what over, Joe, I mean, Maggie?

MAGGIE: I need a flood. I need the Mississippi River to flood. I need to get into a lousy relationship. I need to take a risk. I want to go through with it tonight.

JOE: What flood?

MAGGIE: A poet needs a flood in her life, a Mississippi River flood for a metaphor, to use to write about. You know, the mud and million year old rocks you see after a flood. I need to suffer then write about it like it was a flood. I need to have a bad or good marriage to write about. And I need to be poor. I need to be hungry. I need to marry a bum like you, Joe, to have some sort of real life.

JOE: What are you talking about?

MAGGIE: I have never been more determined in my life. Even more determined than the time I wanted to start a radio station where people could read poetry over the air twenty-four hours a day, and I could play the music I wanted to hear like Sinatra The voice. The chairman of the board.   I'm talking about Frank Sinatra from the late forties and the fifties. That was real Sinatra, I tell you! All Sinatra radio, all the time, and all poetry radio and all plays and people reading novels right there over the air. Everyone would write about Sinatra and the rotten things he stood for, and the decent things he stood for. All poetry and all, skinny guy with a damn good voice and a bow tie. I'm talking about old Indian walking trails, crisscrossing every forest in North America, and old Indians reading Indian poems and singing!

GARY: Poetry on the radio?

MAGGIE: Wait a minute! I have a better idea. All Walt Whitman Poetry Radio!W.A.L.T.

Our Motto: "I am Walt Whitman, as liberal and lusty as nature!" All Walt Whitman poems, all the time, and any poems I want to read or hear and any poets I want to read on my radio station, W.A.L.T.   And furthermore, Joe, this engagement party is real.   We are actually going to go through with it this time!

JOE: You mean it.

MAGGIE: Yes. It.

JOE: Not it?

MAGGIE: It.

JOE: But it's good like it is.

MAGGIE: But that part is over now. Every part has to be over some time.

JOE: It's not over just because you say it is over. We have a deal. I like the radio idea. A radio station with guts. I can read my news stories, right on the air.   But the other thing....the engagement thing. It's a good arrangement.

GARY: What happened up there?

FRANK: *(Enters. With Maureen.)* Looks like you're through boys. Amelia's putting her foot down. She's putting the kibosh to all the nonsense.

JOE: What nonsense?

MAGGIE: Oh why, oh why does everything need to make sense?

GARY: Nothing makes sense in this house.

JIMMY: Never mind that! Maggie! What was that other thing? The Simone thing!

MAGGIE: This is bigger than any crazy radio station idea. I'm talking about a flood!

MAUREEN: Frank and I are ready and we are going now. We are doing the thing we are supposed to do. You see, I say the things I am supposed to say. I know how to live in this world as it is. I know how to act and dress in this world. I am part of it. I am a perfect, beautiful part of this world. Frank and I are going to the O. Henry room of the Iroquois Hotel for our engagement party.

MAGGIE: Now just a minute! I'm a beautiful, perfect part of it too you know!

MAUREEN: Frank and I are not getting married just for ourselves, but for mother as well. You see, unlike you, I know and realize and believe and think that one gets married, not just for oneself, but for one's mother and for society and for the world!

AMELIA: *(Enters having just heard Maureen's speech.)* Yes. Maureen is doing the correct and proper and right thing and I, for one, am delighted and proud of her. I see life simply, you see. You girls complicate it all. When I met your father my late departed husband Harris J. DuMont the third, I was a Copa Girl at the Copacabana Club and I had good legs, you see, and…

AMANDA: *(Enters and she is dressed and ready to go.)* I want to run a cheer leading squad, yeah, that's it. In my cheer leading squad the girls don't do nothin'. See, they just stand around on the side lines in their little skirts and tight sweaters and they light cigarettes and smoke 'em and stamp 'em out right there in the grass; and then light up another one. My cheer leaders chain smoke. They don't even watch the game. Every now and then they flip up their skirts for the boys. That's what they do. Sometimes they drink coffee out of paper cups. They eat bologna sandwiches on white bread and like it when the team loses. Come on, Gary. I'm feeling like some nonpareils and peanuts. We can pick them up at your crummy little store on the way to the O. Henry.

GARY: Huh? Did you call me, Gary? Did you actually say my name?

AMANDA: Yeah, let's pick up the candy and have sex on that little cot in the back room. What do you say? Are you up for it?

GARY: Aaaaa...

JOE: What did she say?

AMELIA: I had three things going for me when I was a girl.

MAUREEN: I am ready, Frank. As ready as I will ever be. This is the moment, my darling.

FRANK: All right, darling. What three things, Mrs. DuMont?

JIMMY: Excuse me, Mrs. DuMont, may I use your telephone? Reggie, where is the telephone?

AMELIA: Reggie, bring the telephone in for Mr. Mahoney.

REGGIE: Very yes, ma'am, sir, Ms. DuMont. *(Exits)*

GARY: O-O-Okay, Am-m-m-manda....

AMANDA: Call a cab, Reggie. Where did she go?

JIMMY: To get me a telephone. (*Yelling to Reggie who is off stage.*) And bring a telephone book while you're at it!

JOE: Having second thoughts about that stupid musical, *The Last of the Mohican.*

JIMMY: Shut up. Now, Maureen, you seem like you have your head on straight... I want you to listen to me very carefully.

REGGIE: Telephone, ma'am.

JIMMY: Thanks. Telephone book!

REGGIE: Telephone book, sir.

JIMMY: Are you listening to me, Maureen? (*He speaks as he rifles through the telephone book.*) Maureen?

MAUREEN: Frank, hearing mother's stories is not in my plan. My plan is to go when I am ready. I am ready. You must seize the opportunity of readiness. When a girl says she is ready—she is ready.

MAGGIE: Take Simone for instance for example forthwith. She's always ready.

AMANDA: I'm ready too, Gary. I am ready, willing, and willing.

GARY: Willing?

AMELIA: Three things: I was ambitious. I wanted to get ahead; to go somewhere and be something. My father was a shoemaker of ladies shoes he smoked a pipe. We lived in Brooklyn. In those days to get out of Brooklyn you could, if you had the legs, get in a chorus in a show on TV. I had the legs. Best legs in Brooklyn. It was my legs that got me my late departed dead husband, Harris McGrady the third, when he was alive, of course.

FRANK: Gee, that's nice, Mrs. DuMont.

MAUREEN: Frank!

FRANK: Hold on, Maureen. We'll go. What else, Mrs. DuMont.

AMELIA: Well... Oh, Reggie, martini, please. Oh, and Reggie....

REGGIE: I know, just *think* about vermouth, sir, Ms. DuMont.

AMELIA: You mean, *Mrs.* DuMont, sir...I mean, ma'am.

REGGIE: Whatever you say Ms. Ma'am, sir.

JIMMY: (*As he looks through the telephone book.*) R. R. Romeo. No, no, no. A. L. Alfa. Now, look, Maureen, you know your sister, Simone, right?

MAUREEEN: Are you speaking to me? Do I know you? Do you realize who I am and the event that is about to take place in my life?

AMANDA: What are you asking her for? I'll tell you anything you want to know. I been reading the encyclopedia and I know everything there is to know about everything. I know all about the International Years Of The Quiet Sun, otherwise known as I.Q.S.Y. It was a program spanning the years 1964 and 1965. Did you know that this program was designed "to investigate the nature of and inter-relationships between magnetic fields in space and charged particles and radiations emanating from the sun as well as to study the effects of these phenomena on the earth's magnetic field and atmosphere"? Did you know that the study "involved the cooperative efforts of 68 countries"? Sixty-eight countries! Not sixty-seven. Exactly sixty-eight! And some of them were communist countries too!

MAGGIE: Spanning the years….Spanning the oceans …. Spanning our lives….I love the word "spanning." Spanning the globe…Spanning…spanning….

AMELIA: You see, Mr. Harris P. McGrady, my late departed dead husband was a leg man. A leg man is a man who is particularly fond of women's legs. Seeing women's legs does something to them. They become… Well, Harris grew quite responsive when he saw my legs. You find out what makes a man responsive, you see, and then…well, he responds.

JIMMY: Alfa Romeo! Here it is. Dealerships. Oh, and, Reggie, get me the automotive section of the last Sunday's *Times*. There's bound to be a 1988 red Alfa Romeo for sale. Take a lesson from me boys. When I want something I do whatever it is I have to do to get it! Now, I'll just dial this number…

GARY: It's Friday night. You can't buy a car over the telephone on a Friday night!

JIMMY: Oh, no? You can do anything you want. Friday night is the best time to buy an Alfa Romeo car. You see, that's the difference between you and me, pal. I take action! I live big! That's why I am going to be a rich and famous actor and you are going to run a two-bit nut and candy shoppe.

AMANDA: How about being poor and famous?

GARY: Now just a minute! I intend to open another shoppe, I
mean store on the east side. In fact, I was thinking that after
Amanda and I got married, you know.... Hey, I'm as
ambitious as the next fella! I'm thinking big. Chain Crazy
Nut and Candy stores! Franchising! Franchising and leasing
back, that's the future. Hey, I am with it!

MAGGIE: Poor and famous! I like it. But, hold the famous.
I'll just take the poor. I've dreamed of being poor. When
you are poor you are free. Mother has set us free, Joe. We
are finally free. You, me, Amanda, Maureen, and Simone.
Free as the final good-bye wave to our childhood. As free
as a thousand times dead-broke! Our clothes turn into
tattered rags; our ribs show and our bones grow stronger.
Thank you mother. O storms and madness and flood! The
Mississippi River floods and I am left with nothing! And I
am happy!

FRANK: Excuse me, pardon me? That was a poem, wasn't it, a
metaphorical type thing to make a point, all that poor and
setting free stuff? You didn't mean Maureen, too.

MAUREEN: Frank, darling. I'm hungry.

GARY: Sure that was a poem, right?   All that crap about
thanking mother and all...

AMANDA: No poem. It is true. And I have decided what I am
going to do. My dream, the dream of my youth, the thing I
knew in my heart and soul I was destined to do and be. The
thing the voice in my head told me was the true me.   I want
to be real estate agent. Yes, show and sell houses in some
suburb on Long Island like Lake Success or someplace. I
want to grow my hair and die it a like honey-blonde and
have these big wavy curls in it. And I want to be middle-
aged with bad skin and sores around my mouth and divorced
and skinny and wear short skirts and blouses part way tucked
in and be a nervous wreck and never have any kids. Mother
is giving me the opportunity of this dream come true. Thank
you mother.   Thank you for this grand chance and

opportunity. The chance to truly find out who I am and who I was meant to be.

GARY: This is a joke.

AMANDA: No, Gary. And you have been chosen to be my first husband because Gary Miller is a perfect first husband type of name. Mother has made it clear that if I marry you, you see, you, a little shop keeper, I will be cut off from my inheritance and lose my healthy trust fund. This is a great break for us. It makes me realize just how much I love you and I am willing to sacrifice so that we can suffer and build our lives and fortune together! We will roll up our sleeves and build Crazy Nuts into an empire! Together!

GARY: Together?

AMANDA: Yes, mother's wisdom has thrown me into your arms. Nonpareils and peanuts and love, that is all I need to live and be happy.

GARY: Aaaaa…

FRANK: Mrs. DuMont. There were three things you said you had. What was the third thing?

AMELIA: I'm glad you asked me that question, Mr. Costella. The third thing is the most important of all. It is the one thing that means the most. It is the thing I have decided to give to my daughters tonight, now, as of a few moments ago. It is the one thing that each of them lacked up until now. And it is the one thing that I have always possessed even in times of great tribulation such as when my dear departed, late dead husband…

JOE: Let's talk about Simone.

REGGIE: Beer, ma'am, sir? I'll tell you all about Simone. You want the scoop on Simone? I'm talking the inside dope on Simone.

MAGGIE: The scoop, the dope. I like those words. I'll use them. I like the word road! I'm going down the road. I'm going up the road. As the crow flies. I like that—as the crow flies. I'm coming by crow. Scarecrow. Why don't they call it crow scare?

REGGIE: I was the scarecrow in *The Wizard of Oz.* I was a dancer for thirteen years. Yep. I love to tap dance. I am a musical actress. I love to sing and dance; and you boys are all wet about musicals. But to get wisdom, first you need a roof. Sure, I'll give you the low down on Simone. (*Nobody listens to Reggie when she speaks.*)

JIMMY: Answering machines! Nothing but answering machines! They do that to make you want it more! The third thing! I can't take any chances, see. I have to have all the bases covered. Where's that automotive section, Reggie?!

FRANK: What was that third thing, Mrs. DuMont? The thing for your daughters. I think we should discuss it. Sometimes change ain't, I mean, is not good.

MAUREEN: Frank, let's take the Cadillac to the O. Henry Room. We can stop on the way and neck. Look at my beautiful long, long neck. You may put your lips on my neck.

REGGIE: Here's the tappy on Simone, if anyone's interested. Gimme a cigarette first and I'll spill the beans.

JIMMY: (*Into the telephone.*) Hello! Hello! Is anybody there? (*To the others.*) Nobody's getting the jump on me. I'll get the Alfa Romeo and Simone before any of you! You're not making a sucker out of me! I can figure this thing out myself. Hello! Hello! Another answering machine! Red. Alfa Romeo. 1988. Top down. One other thing. Think. Think. Think!

REGGIE: When everyone is out, Simone rubs herself against everything in the house. She eats meat—raw. She finds spots of sunlight and curls herself up in it. She stretches like a cat. Simone is a cat. A sleek panther. I've seen her pacing in front of the window.

FRANK: Mrs. DuMont, I am certain you agree with me that Maureen has all of the necessary personality traits to meet with your overall and absolute approval. Now, I do not know what you have told your daughters but surely you see

and it is clear to you and you are confident in the fact that
Maureen is doing all of the things that she is supposed to do
and in this regard is very different from Amanda and Maggie
and…

JOE: Shut up! I hear something. Did you hear that? No, I don't
hear anything. I sense something. That's it. I feel
something is going to happen. Something is coming…

*(Simone enters. She is still wearing animal skins and moving like
a cat. Nobody moves or says anything. They are transfixed.)*

SIMONE: Oh, I am restless tonight. My skin is crawling. I am
anxious. I am breathless. My nerves are raw and I am
hungry, hungry. I am in a cage. I am prowling. I prowl. I
need. I am longing. I long. I long for…I want…I need… I
am seething. I seethe. I am drenched. I sweat. I am
sweating. I am always sweating. Sweat dripping off of my
fingers. I cannot catch my breath. I am out of breath. I
breathe. My muscles are taut. My sinews are compact and
tight and soaking. I am dark and brooding and unknowable
tonight. I am searching. I search. I am looking for
something, something… I eat. I drink. I bleed. I am fleshy.
I am flesh. I am flesh pulsing. I pulse. I ache. I ache I am
aching. I am turbulent. Turbulent. I am wounded. I feel my
heart beating under my skin. My skin. I feel every place on
my skin. I am in my skin I feel all of the time. I cannot
sleep in a bed. I need to be on the earth, the ground. I am
from the ground. I keep thinking about that soldier, alone
and bleeding in that World War One trench. I see him,
thirsty, bleeding, cramps in his legs; he punches them out.
Everything is at stake. Death is near him. Death is next to
him. Death is beside him. I see it. I see death. Life. Life. I
see life. Life is there too. The other soldiers have retreated
and forgotten him. It is dusk. He manages to crawl to the
top to see what is around him. He sees death and the stars.
Death and the stars. Stars. And then this is what happens. I,
who have been in the woods, moving in the wild flowers, I,
like an angel, find my way to him and to him I am an angel

because I will do something to him that will bring him life. Life and the stars. Stars. It will be a dream to him. It will be an inevitable, beautiful dream. I, in my animal skins and he in his ragged uniform, torn and bloody. His face is wet and my face is wet and I press my face to his and press my lips to his and he is dreaming this, we are both dreaming this, I am dreaming this, and it is real. It is not a dream. Dream. Dreams, There is a cool, perfect spring wind. The seasons do not know that this is World War I. The wind is like our spirits, we do not know where it comes from or where it is going but it is here, this cool, cool, wind on our hot wet faces and lips and tongue and places. I look at his wound. The prospects of life rises and rises and shapes and shape in both of us. And it happens like a dream shapes touch shapes and night and stars and ground and the earth and rivers and blasts and blasts of woman and man and man and women and life and life and rivers and stars and flashes of flashes of blasts and life and night and I breathing in the skin and sweat and blood and dirt of him and me steaming. Steam from my head in the stars, and it is all this life in the fields of death and I get all of the life and it is mine and I have it now and he is dying and living as dead and as alive as it is possible to be in the same moment. Death. Life. Death. Life. Night, stars and blood and it is through when I am through and done and finished and complete when I am done and finished and complete and we breathe together out of breath together; we cannot catch our breath together. Breathing, breathing, breathing. I cannot catch my breath. I crawl, climb, my hands and bare feet clutch the earth, the dirt, the ground. I am out of the trench. I look back in the trench at the World War One soldier. He is out of breath. He cannot catch his breath. I look at his wound, the blood. I am out of breath. I cannot catch my breath. I run. I run into the woods, into the forest of the night. Night and life and stars and stars. I search. I am searching. I search. I search...*(Her voice trails off as she exits. The others watch her go. The men splash*

297

*drinks in their faces. They are in shock and no one speaks
for awhile.)*

MAGGIE: You think you can control that or own or have a
piece of that? I might write poetry all right but that was
poetry. That is life! Ripe! Real! Nobody's shoving that
into a wedding dress and dragging her to some hotel room!

JOE: *(Leaping up and grabbing Jimmy.)* You went on dates
with that!? How can you go anyplace with that! That, that,
whatever it is, is too much for you, I tell you! It's too much
for any of us! You can't take her away from us, Jimmy!
You can't do that to your fellow man! We need Simone!

JIMMY: I'm going after her. I am going to find her.

JOE: No!

JIMMY! Yes. I am that wounded soldier.

MAUREEN: Frank. Here is my neck. You may place your lips
there. Right there on my neck. My neck is ready for your
lips, Frank.

FRANK: Believe me, Jimmy, she ain't interested in any Alfa
Romeo car. I know women. You don't have to worry about
the Alfa thing.

GARY: You can forget the ring, too, pal. What was that about
the cot, Amanda? You were talking about that cot…

MAUREEN: Frank. Lips. Here. Now. Neck. Ready.

AMELIA: For some reason, Simone has always seen the
romance in World War One. That Simone…I'm not sure
where she came from…

JIMMY: This is it boys. Wish me luck. I'm heading out. I am
going to find her. I am girding up my loins. This is a war. I
am that soldier and I am ready to do my duty. A man has to
do what a man has to do, to do…and I am man enough to do
what a man has to do, to do. I am going to make the
sacrifice, boys! For God, Country, and Humanity!

JOE: I'm begging you, Jimmy! You're too young to die!

FRANK: Joe's right. You can't go out there. You'll never
make it. I know women.

JOE: That's not a woman! Don't you get it? It's…it's…it's…*a thing*!

MAUREEN: Frank. I am waiting. My neck is waiting.

FRANK: Mrs. DuMont, Maureen, she's normal. Look at her neck. You can't do this to her, because she loves me.

AMELIA: I don't know what you are talking about, Mr. Costella. I am building character in my daughters. They will learn and know what it is like to be poor and to work and have to be like everyone else in the world. They will be hungry, hungry, I tell you. Hungry and penniless in this cold, cold world.

MAUREEN: Lips. Neck.

JIMMY: Good-bye. Farewell. Adieu. "I go. I go. See how I go, straighter than the arrow from the Tartan's bow."

JOE: Then there's nothing we can say to stop you.

JIMMY: Nothing.

GARY: *(Shaking Jimmy's hand.)* Good luck, Jimmy, kid. I know you can do it. I got confidence.

JIMMY: Thank you.

FRANK: All right, Jimmy. You got guts, kid, real guts. *(He shakes Jimmy's hand and pats him on the back.)*

JOE: You are a better man than I am Gunga Din. *(He shakes Jimmy's hand.)*

JIMMY: Thank you, men, thank you. I am ready! "The face of the Great Spirit has come out from behind a cloud. His eye is turned toward me now. His ears are open. His tongue gives the answer." *(He exits.)*

MAUREEN: Frank. Neck. Lips. There.

FRANK: Maureen. My lips. They need reassurance. It's not the money. It's the family harmony thing. Yeah, yeah, that's it. Family harmony. I gotta' know there's harmony in the family.

AMANDA: Forget the cot, Gary. Let's do it in the back of a taxi cab! Let the meter run and fly up and down Manhattan!

GARY: Frank is right about harmony. It's important that you are on good terms with your mother, Amanda. Harmony, that's all we want, isn't it, boys?

AMANDA: Harmony! Ha! That's a laugh. Yeah, yeah, yeah, like money has anything to do with family harmony? You want the money, pal, admit it! Mother doesn't mean it anyhow, boys, so keep your shirts on. She's been making threats like that for as long as...

MAUREEN: Mother. Tell Frank. There's harmony.

AMELIA: Yes, dear. There is harmony. I am resolute, resolved, settled on my decisive intent. I must save my children from themselves and the men who want them for their money which they no longer have, that is if they marry you young men...boys...chaps...fellows. There is harmony now.

MAUREEN: She doesn't mean it, Frank.

AMELIA: I mean it.

MAUREEN: No you don't.

AMELIA: I mean it.

MAUREEN: You don't mean it.

AMELIA: I said, I mean it and I do.

MAUREEN: You don't

AMELIA: I do.

MAUREEN: Mother.

AMELIA: I'll prove it. Reggie, get my attorneys Herrick, Herrick, and Herrick on the telephone.

REGGIE: You bet I will, Mrs. DuMont.

AMELIA: I'll speak to Herrick. I'll show you; all of you. Nobody pushes me around. I mean it this time.

FRANK: Mrs. DuMont, be reasonable.

AMELIA: Reasonable? I'll be reasonable. I'll be the most reasonablest person in the world. Actually, no, now is precisely the time for me to forget reason. I'm through with reason. I'm throwing reason out the window. Sometimes a situation calls for unreasonablity. And believe me, I can be just as unreasonable as the next fellow.

MAGGIE: That's telling them, Mother, kid. I say we will have no more reason. Things just is—are, reasons got nothing to do with it—anything. I figured it out. I'll tell you what we're going to do...

MAUREEN: You are bluffing, Mother.

AMELIA: You'll see if I'm bluffing.

MAUREEN: I don't believe you. Mother.

AMELIA: Oh, you don't believe me? Is that so? Reggie! My lawyers!

REGGIE: I believe her. She means it. I can tell. I know women. I know people. Knowing people is, are, my business. I am a student of human behavior! Now if those humans will just behave themselves...

GARY: That's right. You're an actor. Didn't you say you were an actor? Hey, ever do those theater type acting games? They're fun. I did them in an acting course once.

REGGIE: What did you say?

GARY: Don't you think we love your daughters, Mrs. DuMont?

REGGIE: Wait a minute. What was that thing about theater games?

GARY: What? Oh, yeah. I love those acting theater games.

REGGIE: You are an idiot. Acting is an art! Art! Art! I act in plays and to learn to act in plays, to live truthfully with passion and emotion and conviction and belief, one must act in plays. There is no other training. And if there are no plays to act in, you might as well go to college. Did Edwin Booth play theater games? Did John Barrymore or Ellen Terry or, do you think in that little nut shoppe brain of yours, that that great, great actress, the greatest natural actress of all the history of the world, *Eleonora Duse,* played theater games!? The Greeks! The Greeks! The Greeks and Shakespeare are the things you must play. I am Antigone, and as Antigone I say this to you! "You have made your choice, you can be what you want to be. But I will bury him; and if I must die, I say that this crime is holy: I shall lie down with him in death, and I shall be as dear to him as he

301

Dan Sklar

to me. It is the dead, not the living, who make the longest demands: We die for ever…" That's Sophocles. No little theater game can do anything to that, pal!

GARY: I was just saying…

REGGIE: Shut up! "O, what may man within hide, though angel on the outward side!" That's Shakespeare. And that goes for all of you! Acting! Listen to this poem, it's the only acting lesson there is, and it is written by that great, great poet, Margaret L. DuMont…

MAGGIE: Hey, that's me!

REGGIE: "I dreamed I acted with Edmond O'Brien. We had drinks. His black suit shined like his puffy red face. He looked like tragedy was his brother. In silence his voice resounded. Each drink he took was like sips of sadness'. His countenance was black. His looks at me were sharp judgments cold with compassion. 'You want to be and actor, lay your life on the line, understand! Open your eyes with razors, grab your heart and squeeze it, cry and laugh at the exact same time, don't say a word unless you mean it, say it softly until there's no choice and you have to cry it out. Shut up and listen, be quiet and talk,' he said to me. I dreamed it was like acting with a bolt of lightning; a solid piece of emotion as sharp and controlled as stars. His breath was warm with whiskey, he smelled like corned-beef, Wildroot hair tonic, Aqua Velva, shirt starch and wind from the north through pine trees in August."

MAGGIE: Did I write that?

REGGIE: And now I say to all of you that Mrs. DuMont means it this time because I can see it, hear it, feel it. I know because I am an actor, because I am a woman.

AMANDA: She's a women all right.

REGGIE: Oh, sure I can dance and sing and be charming, but I know how to shine from within me. Mrs. DuMont, I hereby turn in my apron!

AMELIA: Reggie?!

REGGIE: "Truth is truth to the end of reckoning!" That's Shakespeare. This is my destiny!

JOE: What destiny?

REGGIE: My destiny to be on the stage! The theater is my destiny!

JOE: Beer is my destiny!

AMELIA: This is so sudden, Reggie.

REGGIE: Sudden, Mrs. DuMont, sudden? Life is sudden. Suddenly fate has taken its course. That boy, that actor, that Jimmy Mahoney, he can never have Simone. But it doesn't matter because I can play Simone better than Simone. "Oh, I am longing, longing, dripping, dripping, drenched, drenched." And that boy, that actor, that Jimmy Mahoney, he will put me in that play. I will be Alice, one of the brave, beautiful daughters of Munro in *The Last of the Mohicans*.. And I will say things like: "So, Le Renard says he will release all of us if my sister Cora becomes his wife. The thought is worse than a thousand deaths! It would be better to die as we have lived, together!"

AMANDA: Oh, brother.

REGGIE: I will exit to find *my* wounded soldier and take him from Simone. That is my destiny!

JOE: That's a weird destiny.

AMANDA: My destiny, I see it now. I know it! My destiny is to have an office. Yes, an office that I can go to every morning and look out the window at a graveyard; and have pictures of steamboats on the walls. And sit at my desk and look at paper with writing on it and every now and then get angry about something. I'll need someone to yell at about it so I'll hire another person and…

REGGIE: I shall return with Jimmy, and he will be mine!

FRANK: There she goes.

GARY: That was some exit!

AMELIA: I'm delighted.

AMANDA: I'm disgusted.

JOE: I'm thirsty. What about beer?

MAUREEN: Frank, I'm hungry. My mouth wants food and my neck wants lips.

FRANK: Just a minute, Maureen. Well, boys, the scare is over. If Reggie thinks she knows people, she don't. She's a fruitcake.

MAGGIE: Fruitcake, eh? You say Reggie is a fruitcake. I like it. There aren't enough fruitcakes around here. And it's about time some of us rubbed off onto her.

FRANK: Nothing to worry about Maureen, you're right. Shall we...

MAUREEN: Worried?

FRANK: I mean about your mother. Now that Reggie's gone, she can't call her lawyers, Herrick, Herrick, and Herrick.

MAUREEN: Really, Frank?

FRANK: Really. My lips are ready too. Let's get a cab to the O. Henry room of the Iroquois Hotel and I will show you what my lips can do.

MAUREEN: Oh, Frank. You're so romantic...

FRANK: I try. I know women. So long everybody. See you at the O. Henry. (*They begin to exit.*) Wait a minute, Maureen.

MAUREEN: What is it Frank?

FRANK: I just want to think about Simone....All right.

MAUREEN: You may kiss my hand and up and down my arm on the way.

FRANK: I'll start now.

MAUREEN: Oh, Frank...

FRANK: Maureen...

MAUREEN: Yes, right there, that's good... (*They exit.*)

MAGGIE: Ahhh romance...

AMELIA: Someone get me Herrick, Herrick, and Herrick!

MAGGIE: Romance mother. Romance is the thing.

AMELIA: Romance? But isn't Frank Sinatra dead? Didn't romance die when Frank Sinatra died?

MAGGIE: But he's alive, Mother. Frank Sinatra is alive! And even if he was dead, Simone is alive. You can't kill romance. Romance. I love the sound of the word.

Romance.... Romantic.... Two people staring into each others eyes...

JOE: Drinking beer together...yes...yes...it's beautiful.

AMELIA: You can't kill romance, but you certainly can create it, and sometimes romance has to be nudged along a little. Shall we go, children?

AMANDA: Yes we shall, but Gary and me will take our own private, personal taxi. I need sex and I need it now. And afterwards I need nonpareils and peanuts. All that stuff Simone said has made me hungry as heck. Come on Gary, you've got work to do!

GARY: Work! *(They begin to exit.)* What about Simone and Reggie and Jimmy and...

AMANDA: Who cares! *(Grabs her encyclopedia and Gary and they exit.)*

MAGGIE: Buster Keaton! That is it! I want to run a movie theater, yeah, where all we show is Buster Keaton movies. Twenty-four hours a day, nothing but Buster Keaton movies with Buster Keaton running and climbing all over that train and being chased by a thousand women.... And this theater will be in Michigan or someplace and people will come from all over the world and not worry about when the shows are because it will be Buster twenty-four hours a day. And we will watch it, you and me Joe, and there will be plenty of beer because I know that you are in the beer stage of life and beer is important to you.

JOE: What about, Simone? Simone is important to me, just as important as beer, well, almost as important...

MAGGIE: But I am Simone. I will be Simone. When we are alone, Joe, I can out Simone, Simone!

JOE: Okay, poet. When?

MAGGIE: Now.

JOE: Here?!

MAGGIE: A room at the Iroquois Hotel!

JOE: A room?

MAGGIE: That's right Mr. Fiancée! A room! A room with a radio!

JOE: A radio?!

MAGGIE: Come on, Joe! I love the name Joe! *(She grabs him and as they exit he says:)*

JOE: Good-bye Simone! Good-bye Mrs. DuMont. Good-bye Simone…

AMELIA: There they go. Good-by Mr. Hennesse.
(Reggie drags Jimmy across the living room. And as they exit she shows Amelia the ring on her finger.)

REGGIE: I got the ring and I got my Jimmy, Mrs. DuMont! Believe me, I know men! We'll see you at the O. Henry Room of the Iroquois Hotel!

JIMMY: *(As he is being dragged out.)* I was this close. I almost had her in my hand. Simone! Simone! How did this happen? Oh, well… Good-bye Mrs. DuMont…*(Reggie and Jimmy exit.)*

AMELIA: *(Hollering after them.)* Reggie, call me a taxi cab! Fix me a martini! Get me Herrick, Herrick, and Herrick on the line! Oh gosh. Gee. Oh, well. I make a better martini anyway. She thought a bit too much about the vermouth. Simone! If you can hear me, I'm going now. I will be at the O. Henry Room of the Iroquois Hotel at the engagement party of your sisters…I think…I hope…Oh, well. *(Exits.)*

SIMONE: *(Enters immediately.)* Free…Alone and free. I will go to the theater. Yes, off to the theater to sit alone in the back row in the dark. There is a play, *Two Soldiers in Battle*, a Civil War saga. Yes, I will find one of those soldiers deep in the woods, wounded, thinking of me. Good-bye furniture. Good-bye house. And good-night and good-bye to you, audience. I am searching. I search. I long. I pine and moon for something, something, something… Love. Love. Love…

CURTAIN

306

About the Author

Dan Sklar's work has been most recently published in *The New York Quarterly, American Jones Building and Maintenance, Paper Boat Magazine, ProCreation, Kimera: A Journal of Fine Writing, Sightings, Modern Haiku, Tight, Fan, Nebo: A Literary Journal, The Baybury Review, Writer to Writer, Orbis, Curbside Review, Chase Park, Wavelength,* bowWOW, the University of California's, *Into the Teeth of the Wind,* and *Urban Spaghetti.* His book, *Straightforward: Plays, Poems, Stories,* was published by Simon and Schuster in January 1998. His plays have been seen Off Broadway and throughout New England. His play, *The Day Frank Sinatra Died,* was performed by the Endicott Players in the spring of 1998, and in November by the Playwrights' Platform group in Boston. Dan was the featured poet in the spring creative writing series at Salem State College and read his work there on March 8, 1999. His play, *Siberian Women and the Red Moon* was performed by the Endicott Players in April 1999. His short story "Scotch and Love and Adultery" appeared in *The Baybury Review* in the summer 2000 issue. He teaches writing at Endicott College and lives in Salem with his wife, Denise, and two sons, Maxfield and Samuel.

Printed in the United States
3947